THE GUNFIRE

Glancing around, Yovana could see everyone was down. The enforcers lay sprawled on the concrete. It was a massacre.

A tall, dark-haired man dressed in black stepped out from behind the row of parked cars. He was alone. One gunman had defeated six, all in the space of a few heartbeats.

His long unbuttoned coat flapped as he came toward her, submachine gun in hand. Between the lapels of his coat, she could see the webbing of a combat harness, and under that, an armored vest.

At least her death would be quick, she thought. And as he loomed over her, she said one last prayer for the safety of her children.

"Get up," the dark man said in English. His blue eyes were like ice. "Come on," he said, shifting the weapon to his left hand and offering her his right. "We don't have much time."

MACK BOLAN ®

The Executioner

DON PENDLETON'S
THE EXECUTIONER®
NIGHTFIRE

Lord of the Seas
Trilogy
Book I

A GOLD EAGLE BOOK FROM
WORLDWIDE®

TORONTO • NEW YORK • LONDON
AMSTERDAM • PARIS • SYDNEY • HAMBURG
STOCKHOLM • ATHENS • TOKYO • MILAN
MADRID • WARSAW • BUDAPEST • AUCKLAND

First edition June 2000
ISBN 0-373-64259-8

NIGHTFIRE

Printed in U.S.A.

You will not be cold, Mama. You will not be hungry.
Dearest Mama, I will take the risk to give you the gold.
> —*Los Crimenes d'amor* by *El Corazón Fuego*

I often think about the cost of the long campaign, the family and friends I have lost forever. Over the years I have learned that the Sword of Justice has two edges— both razor sharp. To fear one is to fear the other. I fear neither, and I mourn.
> —Mack Bolan's war journals

THE
MACK BOLAN®
LEGEND

Nothing less than a war could have fashioned the destiny of the man called Mack Bolan. Bolan earned the Executioner title in the jungle hell of Vietnam.

But this soldier also wore another name—Sergeant Mercy. He was so tagged because of the compassion he showed to wounded comrades-in-arms and Vietnamese civilians.

Mack Bolan's second tour of duty ended prematurely when he was given emergency leave to return home and bury his family, victims of the Mob. Then he declared a one-man war against the Mafia.

He confronted the Families head-on from coast to coast, and soon a hope of victory began to appear. But Bolan had broken society's every rule. That same society started gunning for this elusive warrior—to no avail.

So Bolan was offered amnesty to work within the system against terrorism. This time, as an employee of Uncle Sam, Bolan became Colonel John Phoenix. With a command center at Stony Man Farm in Virginia, he and his new allies—Able Team and Phoenix Force—waged relentless war on a new adversary: the KGB.

But when his one true love, April Rose, died at the hands of the Soviet terror machine, Bolan severed all ties with Establishment authority.

Now, after a lengthy lone-wolf struggle and much soul-searching, the Executioner has agreed to enter an "arm's-length" alliance with his government once more, reserving the right to pursue personal missions in his Everlasting War.

PROLOGUE

East Cape, Baja California

As the twenty-three-foot open boat pounded through the wind's chop, Mike Croft tipped back the brown beer bottle and gulped cold Pacifico between the rhythmic impacts. Croft was glad the Panga was moving, the faster the better. Though barely ten o'clock in the morning, it was already hot enough on the Sea of Cortez to make him sweat; every time they stopped, perspiration dripped steadily from the hem of his soaked T-shirt onto the scarred fiberglass deck. Beside him on the forward thwart seat, his fishing partner searched the water ahead, cupping his hand to shield his sunglasses from the side glare. In his long-billed canvas cap, with three days' growth of grizzled stubble encrusted with salt, Bob Young looked like a pint-size Papa Hemingway.

"Boat!" Young shouted, pointing at a white speck and windshield flash near the horizon. The other Panga appeared to be slow-trolling off the lighthouse, which stood on a bluff on the desert coastline three or four miles ahead.

Croft glanced over his shoulder at the skipper. Standing at the tiller of the Mariner seventy-horsepower outboard, Ismael remained stone-faced.

"Are they working the spot we're headed for?" Croft asked their fishing guide.

Ismael shook his head once, minutely. He was a man of

concise gestures and few words. His words got even scarcer if the fishing was poor, as it had been so far this day. It was clear to Croft that Ismael didn't think much of fly-fishers. Earlier in the morning, when neither of his passengers had been able to push a cast far enough to reach a sailfish sunning on the surface, he had made no effort to conceal his contempt.

Because Croft's Spanish consisted of a few phrases learned from a $1.25 *Spanish for Fishermen* booklet, he couldn't explain the difficulty of driving a heavy, air-resistant fly more than eighty feet. With a tailwind it was a bitch, with a head wind it was close to impossible. On top of that, flailing the stiff, blue-water fly rods back and forth in one-hundred-degree heat drained the strength out of arms and back in short order. Even if Croft's translation skills had been up to it, he doubted that their guide would have been interested in an explanation. Ismael's attitude was, why go to all the trouble when you could chuck out live bait on conventional fishing gear and get an immediate hookup? In other words, *mosqueros* were loco.

Croft couldn't argue with that.

Bob Young let out another shout, jabbing a finger at a line of widely spaced, floating objects a hundred yards off the port bow. The orange Styrofoam blocks were tethered to each other with yellow nylon rope. As they approached the floats, he told Croft, "We need the wind behind us. Better remind him again."

Croft turned to the skipper, got his attention and indicated his own back with a thumb. *"Viento aqui,"* he said.

Ismael signaled for silence with a curt, horizontal slice of his hand. Dropping the boat speed to a crawl, he scanned the water along the string of crude buoys that held up the commercial shark net. Croft and Young were at a loss to see any signs of game fish. With the wind up and the sea choppy, it took experienced eyes to pick out the V-wakes of barely submerged tail fins.

"Do you have *dorado* here?" Croft asked him.

"Cast here," Ismael said, shutting off the motor. He dipped a hand in the Panga's live bait well, caught a small, brown-backed bait fish and hurled it in a high arc. It landed on its side with a splash a yard from the net.

At once the sea exploded to life. Even Croft and Young could see the swirls as *dorado* homed in on the hapless bait from all directions.

"Cast! Cast!" Ismael exclaimed, reaching into the live well for more bait.

Young grabbed his rod and scrambled up onto the boat's tiny, unrailed bow platform. He got off two casts and retrieves, Croft managed one, then the surface action shut off.

Just before everything went dead, Croft glimpsed a purple-brown shadow two-thirds as long as the boat sliding past the front of the net. He blinked and it was gone. He immediately dismissed it as an illusion, a trick of light, the chop and his sunglasses.

When he and Young looked back at the skipper, Ismael made a spiraling, "they went down" hand signal.

"What scared them off?" Croft asked.

"Tal vez tiburón. Mucho tiburón aqui. Grandes."

Croft nodded as if he understood. Actually, he could only pick out three words: much, here and big. The word *tiburón* that Ismael had repeated twice, he didn't recognize. Croft translated for Young, whose Spanish was nonexistent. "Ismael says there's big fish here. We'd better get on them before that other boat sees us stopped and crashes the party."

A mile away, their potential competition was changing direction every few minutes, apparently still trolling without success.

"More bait!" Young demanded.

Ismael gave him a puzzled look.

Young pointed at the live bait well. "More goddamned bait!"

The guide muttered something under his breath as he caught a dozen of the little fish in the mesh of the bait scoop. He used the scoop to flip them toward the buoys. When they splashed down nothing chased them.

Croft cast anyway. His fly landed a foot short of the net. He let it sink for a few seconds, then jerked it back erratically. On the third jerk he made solid contact.

"Whoa!" he cried, setting the hook hard. The rod bent into a deep U-shape and there was an unbelievably heavy weight at the far end of his line.

"What is it?" Young said to him.

"Damned if I know," Croft replied, "but it feels dead." As he pumped the rod, winching whatever it was toward the boat, Ismael stepped beside him.

From the bow platform, Young had a better angle of view. "I see it!" he said. "I see color. Looks big."

"Still not fighting," Croft grumbled.

Suddenly the winching got much easier, as if something had broken loose. Then, with fly line still attached, Croft's catch popped up twenty feet from the boat. It was big, all right. Big and inanimate. Thirty inches to a side, the bale was encased in a heat-sealed, off-white shell of plasticized burlap. Croft towed it close enough to read the printing on the top. Block letters read: Chilean Fish Meal. Eperva Aqua Prime. 50 KG. And there was a picture of a bluefish on a plate. Through the outer skin, Croft could see two rows of slim packages inside.

Ismael said, *"Mierda."*

Young stepped down from the bow. "Really think it's fish meal?"

"Only one way to tell for sure," Croft said.

"I cut the line," Ismael announced, hurriedly picking up a rusted fillet knife from beside the bait well.

Croft stuck a big finger in his face. "No way you're cutting my sixty-five dollar fly line. Besides, I want to see it up close." Croft was thinking about the outrageous story this was going to make when he got back home. Since he outweighed the captain by eighty or ninety pounds, he easily blocked him from the action while Young grabbed a long-handled gaff and used it to draw the bale up against the hull of the boat.

"Too heavy, can't lift it in."

"Hand me that other gaff," Croft ordered the skipper.

Ismael shook his head. On the other side of the shark net, some thousand yards away, the other boat had changed direction ninety degrees; instead of running straight away from them it was now turned broadside. "It's no good," he said. "No more gaff. No put in boat."

Croft shoved him aside to get the hook. He stuck it in the other end of the bale and then he and Young hauled it over the gunwale of the Panga, dropping it onto the deck.

Ismael spoke slowly and distinctly, as if to very small children, and there was a pleading edge to his voice. "It belongs to Don Jorge Luis Samosa, the Lord of the Seas. We should leave now. Quickly."

Croft unclipped the folding knife from the pocket of his shorts. His intention was clear.

"No!" Ismael told him. He started to make a grab for the big man's wrist, but thought better of it when he saw the serrated, stainless-steel blade flip open.

Croft slashed through the plastic top in one quick swipe, exposing the inner packages of vacuum-sealed polyethylene. Two layers of double rows of ten. Inside each package was a block of densely compacted green stuff.

"Man, oh, man," Young said, pushing his Hemingway hat onto the back of his head. "It must be forty kilos of marijuana."

Despite Ismael's protests, Croft slid the knifepoint into one of the packages and sliced it wide open. He pinched out a clump of resinous bud and sniffed at it. "Whew, take a whiff of this."

Young sniffed. "Smells like skunk. I wonder what it's

worth? Hey, maybe we could actually turn a profit on this vacation!''

''Forget that. We can't even take it back to the lodge, let alone home on the plane with us.''

''I know, Croft, I know. I was just kidding. But let's not dump it before we snap a few pictures. This is a major trophy. A fly rod world record!''

As they dug cameras from their gear bags, Ismael grew desperate, waving his hands at them, pointing across the water. ''The other Panga,'' he cried. ''Coming this way.'' He yanked frantically on the Mariner's pull rope, and when the engine started, revved it hard in neutral. The outraged bellow got his passengers' attention.

Croft lowered his camera and Young, posing beside the bale with his fly rod, stopped grinning. The approaching boat was a center console with a T-top, and much bigger than Ismael's. It was also *really* fast. At the same instant, the fishing partners both realized that something was about to ruin their day, if not their whole trip: either the police or the owners of the dope were coming to claim it. They hurriedly tipped the bale back into the water. It hit with a splash, sank momentarily, then bobbed back, slashed side up. The kilo that Croft had opened leaked a confetti of dried green leaves, which spread out on the surface in a widening slick.

''Let's go!'' Young shouted at the skipper. ''Let's get the hell out of here!''

But Ismael didn't put the Mariner in gear. The other boat, a twenty-eight-foot Super Panga, circled around the end of the net, a towering rooster tail of spray thrown up by its twin, 250-horsepower Yamaha outboards. It was suddenly clear why Ismael hadn't tried to run—the bigger Panga could do seventy-five miles an hour. The boat had a crew of three Mexican men, all wearing dark blue lifejackets. The guy in the bow stood behind a formidable weapon, flat-black and long-barreled, which was tripod-mounted to the casting deck; when the Super Panga stopped, twenty yards away, he trained its sights on them.

"Holy sweet Jesus," Young gasped. "That's a .50-caliber machine gun!"

"Policia?" Croft asked Ismael.

The guide gave him a pained and incredulous look as he slowly raised both hands in the air.

Guess again, gringo.

The Super Panga's captain and the third crew member gaffed the bale and pulled it on board. When the marijuana cleared the top of the rail, a dozen kilos spilled out onto the deck.

"Please tell me this isn't happening," Young said softly.

The captain barked something to the machine gunner. Hearing his words, Ismael made a sudden lunge for the shift lever. His fingers never closed on it. The .50-caliber roared, belching flame and smoke, and Ismael flew like a rag doll out of the stern of the boat, propelled backward by a dozen through-and-through hits. Slugs slammed the outboard's housing and burst the pair of thirty-gallon, plastic gas tanks. Fiberglass and epoxy from the gunwale and thwarts splintered into shrapnel as the gunner walked autofire toward the bow.

Croft didn't think; he reacted, turning, diving off the far side of the Panga. He swam as deep as he could, then made for the shark net. He was halfway there when a concussion from behind slammed his legs. Heart pounding, he swam faster. Ten feet down, he caught hold of the net and hung there a few more seconds, until he felt as if he had to breathe or pass out. When he surfaced, the sea before him was a wall of flame and black smoke. Ismael's Panga had been blown to pieces. Very small pieces, which burned in the gasoline slick. To his left, beyond the circle of fire, Ismael's corpse floated facedown, arms and legs spread, drifting toward the net. Bob Young was nowhere to be seen.

Before the horror could fully sink in, the Super Panga's bow nosed around the far side of the flames. Croft instantly ducked back underwater. When he came up for air again, the boat was past the end of the net, heading away from him at high speed. Grabbing the buoy's tether, he turned to face the oncoming curtain of flames. Unsure whether he could outswim them, he stayed put.

The gasoline fire burned out before it reached the floats. Gusts of wind flattened and dispersed the oily smoke. It was all over in minutes. Over so quickly, Croft realized, that perhaps no one onshore had even seen it. That didn't matter, he told himself. I can hold on until the shark fishermen come to check their net. All I have to do is hold on.

Then something rolled just under the surface about fifty feet away. A purple-brown shape as big around as four men. And at least fifteen feet long.

Croft clung to the rope, eyes wide in shock and disbelief. Be a porpoise, he prayed. Please be a porpoise.

As the huge animal swam slowly toward Ismael's body, he got a better look at it. He'd seen the movie *Jaws* maybe four or five times over the years, that plus a number of *National Geographic* TV specials.

It wasn't a porpoise.

The great white shark took the corpse in its jaws at the belt line and shook its enormous head, flailing the limp body on the surface, pounding the water to a froth, until it ripped a big chunk of bloody meat out of the belly and back.

Eat it, goddammit, Croft thought. Get your fill, you bastard.

But the shark didn't eat. It spewed out the chunk of Ismael and returned in no particular hurry to the floating corpse. Once again it gripped, then slammed the dead man against the water; it did this over and over, until it finally severed the body in two, tossing the hips and legs over its back. The smell of blood and excrement wafted over Croft, making him gag and turn his face away.

The great white swam leisurely through the debris, its fin, back and nose out of the water. It looked at Croft as it glided past. Before it vanished, their eyes locked. Though the shark's huge pupil was black and doll-like, the eye itself had expression. It said, "I can do anything I want. Anything."

Out of nowhere, a pack of much smaller, blue sharks appeared. They tore into Ismael's torso as it drifted past the end of the net, pulling out intestines, stomach and lungs. A flock of gulls wheeled overhead, shrieking as they dived in for scraps.

Shivering in the eighty-five-degree water, Croft hung on to the buoy's tether with both hands, his deck shoes hooked in the net below. In his heart he knew he wasn't going to make it. The lighthouse on the desert bluff was only two miles away, but it might as well have been on Mars.

In the next instant, an incredible mass and weight crushed him into the side of the net. The great white rubbed its head against him, nuzzling like a cat. Shark skin rasped against his bare legs and his grip on the rope failed. Driven underwater, he was rolled across the mesh.

Then the shark was past him. Croft struggled back to the surface, treading water as he gasped for air. Half submerged, the great white circled lazily back toward him.

And opened its mouth.

Border Inspection Station, San Ysidro, California

WHEN IMMIGRATION and Naturalization Service agent Lowell Keck waved the battered Econoline van over to the U.S. Customs search compound, the driver's only protest was a halfhearted, "Oh, man." Which told Keck that the shirtless, dreadlocked, tattooed, white-boy surfer and his three male passengers hadn't expected to get back in the States without a top-to-bottom inspection. Unless they were even dumber than they looked, they kept the van one hundred percent dope-free. Customs drug-sniffing dogs could root out the tiniest stub of misplaced marijuana roach. And a stub of roach could cost the surfers their van, their surfboards, even their freedom.

This thanks to the Zero Tolerance policy.

If anybody asked how tough the U.S. government was on drugs, Zero Tolerance provided a ready answer: it's so tough that it'll bust you for a single seed. In practice, however, the threat only frightened off amateur smugglers. For years, those with the right connections and the ability to pay hefty bribes rarely got touched, and then, only when it was in their interest. The really big-time Mexican traffickers routinely sacrificed a few small loads a month in order to maintain the illusion of rigorous law enforcement. Needless to say, Customs' dogs never got downwind of the regular shipments.

A very sweet deal all around, until the shit hit the fan.

In a cloud of blue smoke the Econoline chugged over to the search compound and Keck once again had an unobstructed view south, toward Tijuana, Mexico. Scenic, it was not. A frozen river of idling cars and trucks funneled down to the bottleneck of the U.S. border crossing, where a line of gray kiosks and gates completely barred the road. Mexican hawkers walked up and down the rows of stopped vehicles offering cheaply made tourist goods, straw cowboy hats, serapes, plastic bags of undersized oranges and papier-mâché human skulls with red glass eyes.

Keck switched on the green light and the next vehicle, a beige Chrysler compact station wagon, pulled forward and stopped beside his kiosk. He keyed the license plate number into his computer and asked the driver for identification. Keck entered the driver's license number into the system, then walked around the station wagon, peering through the side and back windows, checking for anything suspicious on the seats or floor.

He might as well have had his eyes closed.

Though the INS agent seemed to be all business, completely focused on the task at hand, he was anything but. Keck fought the urge to turn and look at the next car in line, to confirm that it was, in fact, the maroon Sentra he'd been told to expect.

He handed the Chrysler's driver back his license and said, "Welcome home." Keck stepped into the booth and hit the switch for the green light. As he watched his next customer creep forward, he felt an unpleasant, sinking sensation in the pit of his stomach.

Risk had always been part of the game. Lately, the danger level had taken an enormous jump thanks to a crackdown on the U.S. side of the border by a joint FBI DEA task force. With a special investigative unit hunkered down in San Diego, looking under every rock for corruption, the freewheeling days at the San Ysidro crossing were history. Rumor had it that suspensions and federal indictments were pending on a number of veteran INS, Customs and Border Patrol agents, as well as their Mexican drug-trafficker contacts. In the last week, five major drug shipments had been intercepted just north of the border. Rumor was, someone in uniform had already spilled his or her guts.

The nearly new, four-door Sentra stopped on the white line and the driver turned off the engine. Keck stared down at a Hispanic female in her late fifties with a red lipsticked mouth. There was no mistaking Gaspar Vega's mule. She was wearing a pearl necklace, a black-and-white polka dot dress with a white collar and a matching handbag sat on the passenger's seat. The round, brown, female faces changed; the polka dot outfit remained the same.

Keck entered the California license plate number, very much aware of the video camera mounted on the arch overhead. It recorded his every move, his every word. "Where were you born, ma'am?" he asked.

"Bakersfield," she said with a hint of Spanish accent. She passed her ID over to him.

Keck slowly walked around to the back of the vehicle. He was relieved to see it wasn't sagging under the weight of what was hidden in the trunk. The Sentra's rear suspension had been beefed up. A computer search showed the license plate and ID clear of outstanding warrants. Keck could always count on his old pal Vega to do things right. Successful smuggling over the long haul was all about details. No INS or Customs supervisor reviewing the surveillance tape would raise an eyebrow over this one. Not unless some in-house rat had already fingered him as being dirty.

Keck handed the woman her driver's license, smiled and said, "Have a nice day."

She nodded, started the car and drove through the gate.

Keck turned on the green light for the next car to advance. No sirens went off behind him. No squealing tires. No flashing lights. The maroon Sentra rolled up Highway 5 toward San Diego, carrying maybe five million dollars worth of uncut cocaine. A wave of relief swept over him.

He had just earned fifty thousand in untraceable, tax-free cash—money that for the most part was already spent. At age thirty-one, Lowell Keck found himself in a serious bind. He had a pair of trophy-blonde, high-maintenance ex-wives and five young children to support. His puny federal salary didn't come close to touching his two-household bottom line. In the past three years, to cover these expenses, he had turned a similar, selective blind eye a half dozen times. Though Keck still worried about getting caught, the moral consequences of his actions had never really troubled him. That he was doing it for his loved ones was all the rationale he'd ever needed.

Like many of the INS and Customs agents working the border, Keck grew up in the area. He had gone to high school in Chula Vista with Gaspar Vega. They had taken auto shop together, and outside of class had worked on each other's cars. Since graduation, Keck hadn't seen Vega socially. They occasionally bumped into each other at vintage auto and hot rod shows. While the financially strapped Keck had be content window shopping, his high school buddy collected rare cars in a big way.

For the past seven years, Vega had owned and operated the Vega Transport Company, which hauled goods to and from Baja. Not an easy way to get rich quick, if ever, under normal circumstances. But normal circumstances had gone out the window when Customs had instituted the Carrier Initiative Program, a policy of noninspection of certain classes of commercial vehicles as an incentive to cross-border trade. Which of course turned out to be an incentive for the drug cartels to transport in quantity. Before the Carrier Initiative Program was shut down, Vega had made himself a bundle. So had a few lucky border control agents. The payoff for letting a single semitrailer slip through had been as much as $250,000 in cash. That kind of bribe money permanently corroded the system, which was the reason why the FBI and DEA had parked their butts in San Diego.

When regular inspections of cross-border transport trucks resumed, Vega started moving his cargoes in noncommercial vehicles. Smaller payloads meant smaller bribes. Keck never got a taste of the really big bucks.

Timing was everything.

"Where were you born?" Keck asked the next driver. There was still so much adrenaline coursing through his veins that he didn't hear the man's reply. "Can I see your identification, please?" he went on automatically. "How long were you in Mexico?"

FIFTY THOUSAND DOLLARS in used small bills fit nicely into a paper supermarket shopping bag. As he nursed a tropical fruit smoothie on the top-floor food court of downtown San Diego's Horton Plaza mall, Keck visualized just such a bag and its pleasant, substantial weight in the hand. He sat at a white plastic table with a blue-and-white striped umbrella. Bags from Brookstone, FAO Schwartz and Benetton were piled around the legs of his chair. Keck was trying his best to be a good dad to his kids.

As he watched the other shoppers come and go on the hot, sultry midsummer night, he searched for a familiar face. He knew he probably wouldn't recognize the person delivering his money. Vega was very careful about such things. On a much less cheerful note, Keck also looked for signs of an FBI-DEA trap. Given the circumstances, it was possible they had his payoff under surveillance. If that was the case, he knew the Feds might not arrest him the moment he received the bribe. They might wait until after he'd stashed the cash in one of his safety-deposit boxes. Keck pushed the useless, negative thoughts from his mind. Whatever happened, he was in too deep to back out. He needed the money.

Three young, clean-cut, Hispanic men walked in his direction, laughing at some shared joke. They wore upscale, European-looking sports clothes, and each carried a mall shopping bag. When they approached his table, Keck waved them off. "These chairs are taken," he said. "I'm waiting for my friends."

The tallest of the three reached a hand into his bag from The Gap and raised it so Keck could see the small, circular tear in the bottom. Through the tear poked a fat, blue steel cylinder with a small hole in its center. Aiming the sound-suppressed pistol at Keck's right eye, the Hispanic said, "Get up, *Migre*."

The INS man stared at the gun muzzle, too astonished to move. They weren't Feds. Nor was this a random holdup. *Migre* was the Spanish slang for *Immigración*. Immigration. These three knew exactly who he was. Keck's shock gave way to dread, which he tried to cover with anger.

"Who sent you?" he demanded. "What do you want from me?"

"We'll talk about that someplace more private. Get your ass up or I'm going to cap you."

Keck slowly stood. As he did, one of the men ran a hand over his chest and back, feeling for a hidden radio transmitter or weapon. Finding nothing, he gave Keck a shove away from the table. The third man gathered up Keck's packages, then the four of them proceeded across the court, toward the row of stores opposite. If any of the other shoppers noticed what was going on, they did nothing about it. Mall security was nowhere in sight.

They headed for the handicapped restroom The wheelchair access lavatory was locked, but the tall man produced a key. After he opened the door, Keck was forced inside, then into the brightly lit, wide, tiled stall.

These guys hadn't been sent by Vega. He didn't use guns or hired muscle, and certainly not on friends. He got his money from the Murillo brothers' organization, which controlled the flow of drugs up the Baja peninsula; the Murillos in turn were in the employ of Don Jorge Luis Samosa, the self-styled Lord of the Seas, one of the DEA's most wanted international traffickers. If Vega was nonviolent, his employers were anything but. The Murillo organization bragged about the murders of Baja judges, police chiefs, military officers and journalists, as well as competing traffickers. The awful truth dawned on Keck: if these men had been sent by the Murillos, he was about to die.

In the enclosed space, the Hispanic man's cologne was overwhelming. So sweet, he thought he was going to be sick. His legs had gone to rubber. "Forget tonight's payoff," he managed to croak. "You keep it and let me walk away."

"It's already forgotten," said the man with the gun. "The blow never made it to San Diego. Got seized by the Feds."

"Hey, I had nothing to do with that! Where's Gaspar? For Christ's sake, talk to him, he knows me. He knows I wouldn't do anything like that."

One of the men used the toe of his shoe to kick up and tip back the toilet seat and lid. Behind Keck, there was a rustling sound. Before he could turn, the third guy pulled a black plastic garbage bag down over his head and shoulders, plunging him into smothering darkness. As Keck started to struggle, he felt the gun muzzle jam behind his ear.

There wasn't even time for a prayer.

Just a sharp instant of pain, the momentary sensation of falling forward, then oblivion as the tall man emptied nine more rounds from the .22 autopistol into the back of his head.

The hit men left Lowell Keck in a kneeling position, facedown in the toilet, surrounded by his expensive packages.

Tijuana, Baja California

Arturo Diaz half listened as full-volume salsa music surrounded him. Behind him, heavy, ruby leather-upholstered doors swung open and a well-dressed Mexican couple exited the El Zorro Azul nightclub. When the doors closed, the sound level dropped, but it was still loud on the street—so loud the bouncer could feel driving bass and drums though the soles of his shoes.

Two coming out meant two could go in.

Diaz lowered the velvet rope from its stanchion and let the next couple in line proceed to the doorway. He reattached the rope and looked down the queue of maybe seventy-five people that stretched along the sidewalk. The building had once housed dentists and lawyers, but now it was four floors of fun and games for the affluent. Only unimportant people entered through Diaz's door. The ground level was set aside for them. The upper stories entertained very special guests; access was from a private elevator in the building's underground parking structure.

Though El Zorro Azul was packed every night of the week, the club lost money, primarily because it featured the hottest Latin American pop groups. On each of its floors, which were actually separate clubs with different theme decors, big-name bands performed simultaneously. The noise from the floors above and below didn't bother club goers, as each group played loud enough to blot out the competition. Out on the street the effect was musical bedlam. Given the high-priced talent the club showcased, for the place to turn a profit it would have had to seat a hundred and fifty thousand people a night. But its backers, Diaz's bosses, didn't care about the financial drain. Drug money kept the El Zorro Azul afloat.

And there was always plenty more where that came from.

At the far end of the queue, Diaz watched a tall man start down the line toward him. He wore a long, loose-fitting, dark gray overcoat. The coat looked expensive. The man's footwear was definitely expensive. Even at a distance, Diaz recognized the brand: black Mephisto joggers imported from France. The guy had dark hair, cut short. He walked with a relaxed, powerful stride.

Gringo, the bouncer thought.

A big part of Diaz's job was measuring people. For wealth. For threat. People who appeared to have too little wealth or offered too much threat didn't get past him.

Something about the way this guy carried himself rang Diaz's alarm bells and he took a full step out of the doorway to get a better look. As the stranger bore down on him, the two made eye contact for a fraction of a second. Diaz's nostrils flared and his neck muscles tightened, an automatic, involuntary response. He'd never seen the man before, but he knew the breed, all right. Killer knows killer like dog knows dog, from a few drifting molecules of scent.

This killer wasn't on the Murillo brothers' payroll. This killer didn't belong here.

Diaz had an awful, metallic taste in his mouth. Fear. Convinced that his own death—sudden, violent and certain—was a few yards away and closing, Diaz slid his right hand to the small of his back and the walnut-gripped pistol butt sticking up from his trouser waistband. Though he'd practiced the quick draw thousands of times, this time his hand seemed made of lead, his fingers half numb and stiff. Before he could pull the snub-nosed .38, the man in the overcoat was on top of him.

But there was no battle.

The big guy breezed past without a glance, moving down the sidewalk.

"Did you see that big bastard?" Diaz croaked at his partner on the door. Speaking was painful. His throat felt like he'd swallowed a tablespoon of fine sand.

"Huh?" the other bouncer said, turning from the pretty young woman in line he'd been talking to. "What bastard?"

By the time Diaz looked over his shoulder, the man in the overcoat had disappeared around the corner. He hurriedly unclipped the walkie-talkie from his trouser pocket and signaled the garage entrance. "You got a tall guy coming your way," he said. "Looks like trouble to me."

After a short pause, the walkie-talkie's speaker crackled. "I see him," came the reply. "No problem."

Diaz signed off. The two men guarding the garage entrance packed sound-suppressed mini-Uzis, and they weren't shy about using them. If the garage guards whacked the gringo, no way would Diaz or anyone else hear it over the blaring music. The color slowly returned to the bouncer's heavy-jowled face.

He hoped they whacked him good.

To Mack Bolan's left, traffic rumbled over the Tijuana street, raising a cloud of dust. On the sidewalk ahead of him, a wiry Mexican in a black silk sports shirt stepped out around a corner of the drug cartel's nightclub, a corner created by the driveway that angled down under the building to the parking garage entrance. The Mexican held something to his ear, a cellular phone or walkie-talkie. Looking right at Bolan, he spoke into the device, then he disappeared the way he had come.

The man known as the Executioner slipped both hands into his overcoat. In the right pocket, his fingers found a slip of paper; in the left, they closed on the crosshatched, black rubber grips of a .380-caliber Walther. The compact little automatic was good to go, safety off, live round up the pipe.

When he reached the curb where the driveway cut the sidewalk, Bolan stopped and looked right. Forty feet away, a concrete kiosk with a front-facing window sat in front of a door made of heavy-gauge, linked steel plates, which completely blocked the entrance to the underground garage. The two men standing in the kiosk controlled the door. Drug thugs. They watched him intently, their hands out of sight below the window.

Bolan took the piece of paper out of his pocket and glanced at it. Then he turned his back on the kiosk. Across the road, the yellow glow of the streetlights reflected dully in the dirty plate glass windows of one- and two-story commercial buildings. He pretended to search for a street number for a moment, then turned, paper in hand and started down the driveway for the kiosk.

The guards reacted at once, moving to the booth's doorways. They didn't step completely out and their hands remained hidden. The booth's window looked bulletproof. Bolan had to figure the rest of the kiosk was likewise reinforced. A minihardsite.

Under his baggy silk shirt, the skinny guy hid an armored vest. The other guard's clothing concealed nothing; his shirt fit as tightly as a sausage casing. Under the lemon yellow fabric, the vest's shoulder holes and Velcro chest fasteners were clearly outlined.

Bolan's tailor had done a much better job. The extra padding in the shoulders of his overcoat allowed the material to drape smoothly, giving no hint of what was strapped to his chest and waist. ''Excuse me,'' he said, holding out the slip of paper as he approached the kiosk, "can you tell me where this address is?"

The chaotic rhythm of four different songs playing at once, plus the echoes of same off the buildings across the street, made his words unintelligible. The guards could see his lips move, though.

The guard in the silk sports shirt yelled something at him and gestured with the back of his hand. Beat it!

Bolan cupped a hand to his ear. "Sorry, I didn't hear you," he said as he closed the distance.

The guard angrily waved him off, shouting at him first in Spanish, then in English: "Get the fuck out of here!" He and his partner stepped a little farther out of the booth, far enough to display their suppressor-equipped mini-Uzis. Muzzles aiming at his chest.

Bolan held out the piece of paper again. As he did, it slipped from his fingers and fluttered away.

Misdirection was a magician's trick.

Both guards watched the paper fall.

The Executioner leaned forward as if to try and catch it. He dropped into a crouch and his left hand came out of his pocket and up in a blur. He fired the Walther once. The crack of the single gunshot was lost in the thunder of bass and drums. The guard took a .380 Silvertip round under the chin. The expanding slug angled up through the front of his throat, through the soft tissue of tongue and plowed through the roof of his mouth into his brain, where it stopped. As the man's knees buckled, Bolan pivoted.

The other gunner realized what had happened, but before he could line up his Uzi, there was another almost inaudible crack and a finger of flame licked out from the Walther's muzzle.

The hardman took the .380 round just below his nose. His head snapped back violently as his front teeth shattered. The mushrooming bullet veered sharply to the side, exiting in a puff of red at the hinge point of his jaw. Eyes wide with pain and horror, the guard dropped his weapon and clutched his ruined face. He tried to scream, but choked on the blood that filled his mouth and poured from between his gaping lips.

Death came a fraction of a second later, when Bolan put a merciful second bullet through his right eye.

The Executioner stepped over the jerking corpse, leaned into the kiosk and turned the key that operated the garage door. As it rolled up out of the way, he grabbed hold of the fat gunner's heels and dragged the body inside the parking structure, pulling it into a dim corner beside a Dumpster, away from the stark, overhead lights. He did the same with the other guy. The parking garage door he left open. Bolan didn't plan on staying long.

He moved quickly down the aisles of parked luxury cars. Custom Jags. Rolls. Mercedes limos. All polished and detailed to gleaming perfection. As expected, there was no sign of drivers or bodyguards. The cartel's hired help waited upstairs in a special room. When the time came to leave, they accompanied their employers down from the club in the elevator, then escorted them through the garage to the vehicles.

A hit on the private playground of the Murillo brothers was a job the FBI and DEA wouldn't touch with a barge pole. It violated any number of international treaties and laws. It was a job for someone who couldn't be linked to official channels. In the next few minutes, things could go sour in a thousand different ways. There were lots of guns and lots of people in the nightclub above. Some of the people were innocent. Now that the strike was under way, there were no guarantees for anyone.

Bolan unbuttoned the front of his overcoat. Underneath, he wore a black T-shirt and slacks, body armor with full trauma plates, and a ballistic nylon combat harness. He lifted the lanyard loop of his MAC-10 submachine gun over his head. Taped back-to-back to its magazine was an extra

30-round clip. Under his left armpit in shoulder leather hung a Beretta 93-R. Grenades dangled from the harness's chest strap grommets.

As he walked toward the elevator, he tested the compression fit of the screw-on noise suppressor. Then he dropped the MAC-10's magazine into his palm and checked the stack of 9 mm Black Talons. After slapping the mag back in place, he pulled the charging handle and dropped the safety selector switch to auto.

The Executioner was ready.

2

Yovana Ortiz looked at her reflection in the brightly lit mirror of the ladies' room. Under the long eyelashes, the carefully applied mascara, her green eyes radiated panic. Gripping the edge of the black marble-topped counter, Ortiz closed her eyes and forced herself to take a series of slow, calming breaths to still the butterflies batting against the walls of her stomach.

Every actor fears dying before his or her audience, going blank and forgetting a speech, shattering the illusion of a performance. The former Mexican television soap opera star knew if she flubbed a line this time, there would be no stopping the tape, no chance for a retake. She would die for real.

A girl in her late teens, dressed in a red spandex, micro-miniskirt and clunky, disco-style high heels, exited one of the rest room's stalls and stepped up to the mirror beside her.

Though El Zorro Azul's top floor was packed with people, all of them wealthy and connected, all of them drinking quantities of alcohol, there was no line outside this particular rest room door, and no crowd inside waiting to use its elegant, gold-plated facilities. Except for the Latin music, which was so loud it shook the walls, it might have been a powder room in a fine department store. A uniformed, female caretaker decided who could and who couldn't enter this sanctuary. Admittance was a matter of status, and Yovana Ortiz still had plenty of that. In the world of traffickers, their bodyguards, extravagantly gorgeous women and rich hangers-on, she was something of a queen.

Drug royalty.

The girl beside her had straight, silky black hair down to her narrow waist. She wore a tiny, gold lamé purse on a gold chain around her wrist. The girl wiped the residue of cocaine dust off her nose and licked her fingertip. When she placed the tiny glass vial on the counter close to Ortiz's hand, it clicked against the polished stone.

"Have some," the girl said as she examined the state of her glossy, ruby-red lipstick.

Ortiz stared at the tube half full of cocaine.

Narcotics were used openly and freely in El Zorro Azul, despite a high-ranking police presence. Everyone was bought and paid for by the cartel. Including Ortiz. From the time she was fifteen, there had never been a question of her *not* selling out to someone, body and soul. It had always been a matter of holding out for the highest bidder. For a beautiful woman, money was power, and power was protection. From the animals.

Of course, there was a sizable downside. When a pretty woman lost favor with her protector—or betrayed him— the sky itself would fall on her. Ortiz had seen the cracks forming many months earlier. The only way to survive the wrath of a vicious dog was to find herself an even bigger one. And that was exactly what she had done.

"Go on, help yourself," the girl said, nudging the vial closer.

Ortiz couldn't deny that she felt the urge to do some of the coke. She knew it would boost her confidence. But she had given up the drug before she had gotten pregnant with her oldest boy, Juanito. He was eight years old now. She would never go back down that road. Never.

"No, thanks," Ortiz said.

With a shrug, the girl swept the tube into her purse. She

had a baby face, perfect skin and a winning smile. A tight little body. Long, slender legs. All of which were important commodities in this marketplace. The trouble was, new product arrived almost daily. Pure product. And when the new stuff came in, the opened packages got sent down the line, to be recycled through any number of users with increasingly less and less status. In other words, barring a miracle, from here on for this pretty little girl it was all downhill.

Ortiz thought about giving the teenager a warning, but didn't because she knew it wouldn't have done any good. For the moment, the child-woman had the world at her feet. She wouldn't have listened to reason and experience, any more than Ortiz would have listened ten years earlier.

The long-haired girl left the rest room without another word. Ortiz smoothed the skirt of her own skintight, little black dress. She knew if she delayed her return any longer it would only make her more nervous, which would increase the risk. She pinched her cheeks hard to bring up the blood and hide their fear-induced pallor. "This is for Juanito and Pedro," she said to her reflection. "I do this for my children."

Two men were waiting for her when she stepped back into the crush of the nightclub. Tall, muscular guards in gray silk suits. Though always obedient and deferential to her, there was never a doubt to whom the bodyguards belonged. Like her, they were the personal property of Jorge Luis Samosa. Don Jorge, the Lord of the Seas.

The crowd parted for Ortiz's escorts as they led her past the bar and dance floor. A few people nodded as she moved by. And all the others looked thrilled just to be in the same room with her. The bodyguards took Ortiz through the thick, blue haze of Havana cigar smoke to the elevated dais along the rear wall, which held a large, plushly upholstered booth occupied by a dozen people. It was the Murillo brothers' private table, the status summit of El Zorro Azul.

Before Ortiz could slide back into her usual position of honor at the head of the table, a pair of perfectly dressed, beautiful women and their matching male counterparts had to slide out. As they did so, Ortiz sensed that something had changed. During her brief absence, the fiesta had ended.

The only person smiling, the only person who would look her in the eye for more than an instant was Roberto *"El Azote"* Murillo. Roberto "The Whip" sat alone at the far end of the table with his back to the wall. His brother Ramon, nicknamed *"Tres Clavos,"* or "Three Nails," had left the booth and was nowhere in sight. Stocky in build and round-faced, Roberto wore his thinning black hair down to his shoulders in greasy coils. Of the two brothers, he was the more animated and excitable. Ramon always had a sour, bored expression on his long, gaunt face. Dark-skinned and sharp-featured, Ramon appeared to have more *Indio* blood than Roberto. Their mother had been a street prostitute of the lowest grade. It was obvious to anyone with eyes that they had been sired by different fathers.

Roberto and Ramon Murillo were monsters. Totally self-made monsters. As boys, in order to survive, they had sold drugs on corners in Tijuana's slums. When they grew big enough, they started bullying and beating others into doing the selling for them. By the time they were in their early twenties, the Murillos controlled not just Tijuana's drug flow, but the main land and sea transport routes from the southern tip of Baja to the California border. They consolidated and maintained their territory with silver and lead, with millions of dollars in bribes and a private army of murderers.

When the Murillos saw something they wanted, they took it. When they saw something they feared, they killed it. Jorge Luis Samosa appreciated and highly valued both of these qualities. If Yovana Ortiz was a queen in Samosa's international drug empire, the two Murillos were its crowned princes.

The amused expression on Roberto's face alarmed Ortiz, but she took her seat in the booth. There was nothing else she could do.

With a drumroll, the band launched into the next song. The audience recognized it immediately. They sent up a cheer as they began to sway to the slow rhythm. When El Corazon Fuego's lead singer belted out the first words of the verse, the packed house sang along.

Roberto listened for a moment, then pushed to his feet. "Everybody sing," he ordered.

The guests at his table rose and joined in on the chorus of "Crimes of Love."

The song told the story of a young, would-be trafficker making promises to his dying mother in a shantytown shack. The story was widely believed to be autobiographical, based on the early lives of the Murillos. Of course, Roberto and Ramon hadn't been cold or hungry for at least fifteen years. Their own mother had deserted them when they were babies. She had been murdered in an alley a decade ago, her throat slashed from ear to ear by a drunk with a broken beer bottle. "Crimes of Love," a song commissioned, produced and promoted by the Murillos, created and celebrated a past that had never existed.

Which underscored a lesson Ortiz had already learned: The Whip and Three Nails were capable of subtlety as well as brutality. Bankrolling the already successful Mexico City pop group and getting the pro-drug smuggler anthem national radio airplay had been an ingenious and effective public relations move.

Ortiz pretended to sing along with the others. The lyrics were so distorted and perverse they turned her stomach. "Crimes of Love" pandered to the Mexican romanticism of banditry, and to its desperate need for heroes. It said smugglers were like Robin Hood battling a powerful oppressor, the U.S. government, battling to free their loved ones from disease and squalor.

In the most colossal lie there is always a little bit of truth. Even the cartel bodyguards took home three thousand dollars a week.

Of course, in tax-free cash and side benefits, Ortiz was about to give up that much a day. Her pending secret deal with the FBI-DEA task force offered prosecutorial immunity and a new identity, not a continuation of her current lifestyle. She didn't care.

The song's crescendo was greeted with wild applause. When Roberto sat, everyone else sat.

"So, Yovana, how was your shopping in San Diego?" he asked as she sipped iced water.

Her throat constricted, but to her credit, Ortiz didn't cough or sputter. She swallowed, carefully placed the glass on the table in front of her, then dabbed at the corners of her mouth with her napkin. "Expensive. So expensive," she said.

"And your new gringo friends?"

Roberto stared at her without emotion, calmly puffing on his Cuban cigar. How much did he already know? she asked herself. The look on his face revealed nothing. Around the table, the tension was palpable. She could feel her old friends pulling away, distancing themselves from her. And from her fate.

"I don't know what you're talking about."

"You didn't think we'd find out?" Roberto asked.

"Find out what?"

"We've had five major shipments seized in the last week. Did you expect us to write off that kind of loss without looking into it?"

"I still don't know what you're talking about."

Roberto smiled and shook his head. "Money makes the world go round. Did you really think that we couldn't find someone in the FBI or DEA who would sell you out for money?"

"You've made a mistake," Ortiz replied angrily. The mistake, of course, had been hers when she had conceded to the Feds' demands. That she'd given in to them at all was a measure of her desperation. The FBI-DEA task force had wanted a "good faith" gesture from her. They wanted her to bring something concrete to the table in advance of the negotiations for what she really had to sell. She'd objected to the idea of fingering the cocaine shipments because it was so dangerous, but the arrogant bastards had insisted.

Roberto waved off her protest. "My brother and I have put up with much from you," he said. "We've gone to considerable pains and expense because of who you are, but all that's finished. You've crossed the line. There's no protection for you, now."

Ortiz looked at her bodyguards. They wouldn't meet her gaze, either. A very bad sign. Fists balled under the table, she insisted, "I must speak to the Don—"

"He doesn't want to talk to you," Roberto said. "He already knows everything. We used the Internet to send him digital camera surveillance pictures of your shopping spree at Nordstroms. And we positively identified the woman in the adjoining change booth as an undercover FBI agent with the San Diego task force. Don Jorge signed your death warrant via e-mail. He gave us specific instructions as to how he wanted the job done." Roberto reached into the inside pocket of his Italian silk sport jacket. "Would you like me to read them to you? Or would you rather it be a surprise?"

Her back to the wall, Ortiz played her ace card. "If I don't return to the States in seventy-two hours with my children," she told him, "copies of certain materials already on the other side of the border will be automatically sent to the FBI."

"You underestimate us."

In his face she could see that he not only thought he was above the law on both sides of the border, he thought he owned it.

"Get the bitch out of my sight!" he snarled.

Ortiz's former friends scooted meekly from the booth, allowing Murillo's henchmen to reach in, grab her and pull her out. She struggled briefly in their grasp.

"You two," Roberto said to her longtime bodyguards, who watched the mauling with obvious discomfort. "Don Jorge wants you to watch and report back that the job was done right."

Two men glanced at each other. Proof of loyalty was required. If they refused, they knew they, too, would die horribly. Their allegiance was to the money. They stepped in and took hold of her firmly by the elbows.

In a phalanx of six cartel enforcers, Ortiz was led through the club and into the private elevator that accessed the underground parking structure. No one spoke as the elevator car dropped. Surrounded by killers, Ortiz could hardly breathe. A terrible weight compressed her chest. Escape was out of the question. Barter was out of the question. She had nothing left to offer. Not even her body. She knew how Samosa liked his revenge. She had no doubt that all six of them were under orders to use and humiliate her before taking her life.

Ortiz had no one to blame but herself. She had made the wrong choices, repeatedly. She had personally profited from evil. She knew she deserved punishment for her wrongdoing. But her children were innocent. And now, innocent or not, they, too, would pay.

The elevator doors opened. Her bodyguards walked her out and down the wide central aisle between the rows of luxury cars.

They'd traveled about thirty yards when something metallic clattered across the pavement toward them—a small, dark object the size and shape of a baseball. Hands dipped under sport jackets for holstered guns as it spun to a stop ten feet away.

One of the men croaked, "Jesus!"

It was definitely not a baseball.

In the next instant, everything changed. Ortiz saw white. An all-obliterating white that flooded the inside of her skull as the explosion's shock wave slammed her from head to foot. Already teetering in her high heels, she staggered backward into blackness. She regained consciousness with a jolt as her tailbone crashed into the concrete. Ears screaming from the close-range thunderclap, she struggled to open her eyelids and found that she couldn't. Reaching up to her blast-numbed face, she realized with horror that her eyes were already open.

Above her, all around her, volleys of automatic gunfire broke out as the Murillos's enforcers wildly sprayed the garage with lead. She covered her head with her arms as she was pelted by spent shell casings. Almost at once something spattered over her legs from ankle to thigh. Something hot and wet. A body thudded heavily to the ground beside her. Ortiz knew if she wanted to survive she had to crawl away, but blinded and disoriented, she couldn't tell where the hostile fire was coming from. More bodies hit the concrete. She shook her head to clear it, forcing her eyes to focus.

One of her guards crouched before her, protecting her body with his. She saw him jolt, saw the five bullets exit his back. Five gory craters stitched in a line below his shoulder blades; chunks of organ, muscle and bone blown over her head, spraying across the garage floor. The man sat down hard in front of her, bent over at the waist, he clutched the ruin of his chest. His shrill, keening cries ended in a strangled gasp.

The gunfire stopped. The echoes faded away. Glancing to either side, Ortiz could see that everyone was down. The enforcers lay sprawled on the concrete in attitudes of death. The air reeked of blood. It was a massacre.

A tall, dark-haired man dressed in black stepped out from behind the row of parked cars. He was alone. One gunman had defeated six, all in the space of a few heartbeats.

Who could do such a thing? she asked herself. Only an assassin hired by some rival drug lord.

His long, unbuttoned coat flapped as he came toward her, machine pistol in hand. Between the lapels of his coat, she could see the webbing of a combat harness, and under that, an armored vest.

At least this death will be clean and quick, she thought. And as he loomed over her, she said one last prayer for the safety of her children.

"Get up," the dark man said in English. His blue eyes were like ice. "Come on," he said, shifting the weapon to his left hand and offering her his right. "We don't have much time."

3

The petite woman shrank back from Bolan's extended hand, her eyes wide with terror. Surrounded by a ring of corpses, a pond of gore lapping at her heels, she had cause to expect the worst.

"I'm not going to hurt you," the Executioner assured her.

She looked up at him, clearly desperate, hoping against hope that his words were true.

Yovana Ortiz had been gifted with a stunning, exotic beauty. Slender and delicate. As she pulled herself back from the edge of panic, that beauty became little-girl fragile.

"Are you injured?" he asked. "There's blood on your legs."

Ortiz looked down at herself. "It's not my blood," she said. She stared at the twisted, still bodies and shuddered. "They were going to murder me. If you hadn't killed them, they would have killed me." After a pause she said, "Who are you?"

"A friend."

Then came a squealing of tires and the roar of a powerful engine as a heavy car sped into the underground garage.

The woman flinched at the sudden noise, drawing her arms and legs tightly against her body.

"You have to get up," Bolan told her as the gleaming black coupe, its high beams blazing, rushed toward them.

"We have to go, now." He took her small hand in his and helped her to her feet.

"Who are you?" she repeated.

"I'm here to help you escape."

The Lexus coupe screeched to a stop beside them. As Bolan reached for the passenger-door handle, he saw his own face reflected in the impenetrable black of the window's tint. It was devoid of expression, of elation or regret. When he opened the door, the interior light came on, casting a golden glow over the off-white leather upholstery.

The guy behind the wheel was slim and tanned, and he wore his curly black hair cropped short. Jack Grimaldi didn't look over at Bolan or his female companion. Instead, he scanned the killing ground through the windshield's one-way glass, paying particular attention to the closed doors of the elevators. As long as the doors stayed shut, everything was copacetic.

The Executioner tipped the passenger bucket seat forward and hurriedly pushed the woman into the back seat. "Buckle up," he ordered her. "Do it, now."

"Meter's running," Grimaldi said over his shoulder. "Let's move."

As soon as Bolan sat beside him, the former fighter pilot did a number on the clutch and accelerator. The Lexus cut a tire-smoking U-turn on the concrete, slamming the Executioner back into his seat. He managed to get his own safety belt fastened a moment before Grimaldi shifted into second gear.

The fuel-injection engine screamed.

Bolan glanced over at the lighted instrument panel. He could only see the gauge closest to him. The tachometer. Its needle wasn't just in the red—it was pinned to the post.

Getting out of the garage without being seen was the prime directive. And that meant hauling ass. As they whizzed past the entryway and hit the exit ramp's incline, their speed had to be close to eighty miles an hour.

Grinning fiercely, Grimaldi's hands and feet worked in a highly coordinated blur. Almost simultaneously, he feathered the clutch, tapped the foot brake and, steering with one hand, he reached down and grabbed the emergency brake handle, which he then jerked up and locked. The heavy car instantly sank deep into its suspension, and its passengers were squashed into their seats as it flew up the ramp. The locked brakes put the Lexus into a four-wheel, full-out, sideways skid.

Somehow, Grimaldi kept the slide from turning into an out-of-control spiral. He dropped the hand brake, popped the clutch and stomped the gas. Still in second gear, tires shrieking, they bounded out onto the street into the flow of the light traffic.

Third gear. With a sickening lurch, the Lexus accelerated. The buildings on both sides of them grew fuzzy as Grimaldi put one, two, three, four blocks between them and the El Zorro Azul nightclub.

Bolan watched the jet jockey glance up into his rearview mirror, checking for pursuit. Seeing none, he tromped on the brakes again, this time in order to clear a hard right turn. Steering stiff-armed into the wild, four-wheel skid, Grimaldi put the hammer down.

The Executioner let the push of acceleration, a huge heavy hand in the middle of his chest, drive him deep into the formfitting seat. He had absolute confidence in Grimaldi as wheelman, as jet or chopper pilot, and as backup in a firefight. The two men's friendship started at the beginning of time, a thousand battles ago, when Bolan had first declared war on the Mafia.

The face that evil wore had changed often over the years. But it was still the same beast underneath, fueled by the same urges. A beast that could never be tamed or eradicated, only briefly kept in check with lead. And plenty of it. Unlike the narrow, potholed Tijuana street they roared down, the road Mack Bolan traveled had no end in sight.

Though this mission appeared simple enough on paper, limited in scope and time frame, Bolan knew that in the field, events had a tendency to evolve, usually at lightspeed, sometimes in unpredictable directions. He and Grimaldi had been tasked with moving a Mexican national across the U.S. border. If Yovana Ortiz had been just any Mexican national, some official arm of the U.S. government would have handled her transportation. But the woman in the back seat wasn't just anybody. She held the key to bringing down the northernmost tentacle of Don Jorge Samosa's drug empire, an organization that operated with the complicity of high-ranking Mexican government officials and the military. Yovana Ortiz not only knew where all the bodies were buried, she claimed to have the burials on videotape.

In the estimation of the U.S. President and of the Department of Justice's Sensitive Operations director, Hal Brognola, her evidence was of such potential value that no one officially connected with either the U.S. or Mexican government could be entrusted with her protection. What could go wrong, would go wrong. What could be corrupted, would be corrupted. Don Jorge Samosa's bribes had already seriously compromised the drug enforcement communities in both nations. When the word got out that Yovana Ortiz had turned on her longtime benefactor, the price placed on her head would be enormous, in the tens of millions of dollars, and paid in untraceable cash.

Grimaldi made several more sudden changes of direction. Only when he was absolutely sure that they weren't being followed did he proceed toward their real destination.

Bolan turned to look at their passenger. Her breathing was shallow, her eyes half closed. Maybe she was sick from the speed or the jarring turns? he thought. Or maybe it was delayed shock from her close brush with death? Whatever it was, as he stared at her, she surprised him by suddenly snapping out of it. She was much more resilient than she appeared. Or let on. Ortiz was, after all, a trained actress.

"Who sent you?" she demanded of him. "What do you want? Where are you taking me?"

"You can't be adequately protected here, for obvious reasons," Bolan said. "You need to get across the border in order to be safe."

"My children. I won't leave Mexico without them. I don't care about anything else."

"The house where you're keeping them is under discreet, round-the-clock federal surveillance," the Executioner told her. "Your children's bodyguards don't know they're being watched."

"I want my babies with me, or the deal is off."

Grimaldi shot Bolan a look. Hal Brognola had anticipated this complication. Anticipated and had it covered.

Bolan opened the glove box and took out a cellular phone. He hit the Redial and after a pause said, "Striker, here. We have the goods. ETA twelve minutes. We're free and clear. Repeat, free and clear."

Grimaldi drove at moderate speed for another quarter mile, then turned into an empty, corner lot. The headlights picked out clumps of dry weeds, piles of concrete rubble, scattered trash and a beat-up Ford station wagon. He stopped the Lexus beside the wagon.

"The driver will take you to a safehouse on this side of the border," Bolan told Ortiz. "You'll wait there while I go collect your children. I'll bring them back to you myself. Then we'll all cross over together."

"The men who are guarding my boys belong to Don Jorge Samosa," she said. "They will die before they give them up."

"Understood," Bolan said.

"What are your names?"

"Names aren't important."

"You work for the U.S. government?"

"Why don't you just try to relax," Grimaldi suggested in smooth-as-silk Spanish.

As Bolan got out of the Lexus, Grimaldi pulled the trunk-lid release lever. The Executioner removed a large, heavy, ballistic nylon duffel bag from the trunk and lugged it to the station wagon's back door.

With a whir, the rear side window of the Lexus slid down. "Whatever you do, please don't hurt my children," Ortiz said, tearfully. "And don't let the Murillos get them. God, I'm so afraid. Roberto and Ramon are animals. There is nothing they are incapable of. If the Murillo brothers get my children, I'll never see them again. They'll make sure of that."

"They're going to be all right," Grimaldi said. He touched the master switch on his door and the passenger window slid up.

Bolan watched the coupe ease back onto the street and accelerate away, then he slung the duffel in the rear of the Granada.

All four doors of the station wagon were different colors, replacements scavenged from junkyards, as were three of its wheels. It had one original hubcap. For Tijuana, it would blend in.

Bolan climbed into the well-worn front bench seat, which was covered by a tasseled, striped wool blanket. The dashboard's sun-cracked vinyl leaked bits of plastic foam over everything, like yellow snow. There was no key waiting for him in the ignition. He reached under the seat, picked up a pair of needle-nose pliers and jammed them in the already fractured ignition slot. When the soldier turned the pliers, the engine caught at once. He gunned it. It sounded strong.

He switched on the headlights, dropped the transmission into drive and crossed the vacant lot. The street was unlighted, the neighborhood made up of small, blocklike, flat-roofed houses set back from the road. Feeble lights glowed behind their sheet-curtained windows; their dirt lots were enclosed by chicken wire, with fence posts made of dry sticks. The air hung thick with the smell of wood smoke.

Eventually he came to a recently paved road. Ahead, in the glow of mercury vapor streetlights, he could see the cinder-block wall with the gated entrance to the exclusive, hilltop development. The walls and gates were an attempt by Tijuana's wealthy to keep the border-town squalor at bay. Bolan unholstered the 93-R, dropped the safety and laid the autopistol across his lap. As he approached the entrance, he saw the motorized gate was rolled back. He pulled up beside the guard hut and stopped. The hut's door was open; there was no one inside.

So much for security.

He drove on past huge houses, which were decorated with Greek columns and rows of life-size alabaster statuary, dramatically spotlighted for maximum garish effect.

As he neared the corner that led to the cul-de-sac, he slowed to a crawl. He could see both of the joint task force's surveillance vehicles. A blue sedan and a white commercial van were parked on opposite sides of the street. The sedan was the closer of the two and it faced him. He couldn't see anyone inside.

Bolan's plan to circle past the Feds and come at the safehouse from the rear went up in smoke. He swerved the Granada to the curb and, leaving the engine running, bailed out of the car with the Beretta in his fist, held low against the outside of his thigh. He darted down the middle of the street. As he neared the sedan, he could hear soft music. The driver's window was open. Over the sights of the Beretta, he looked in.

The driver lay slumped over the console between the seats, on top of and partially concealing another body. There was a contact wound in the side of the agent's head, the hair matted with blood. The surveillance team had been listening to the CD player when they got hit. It played on, to dead ears. A saxophone requiem by Kenny G.

Bolan dashed past the intersection to the rear of the white van. When he was thirty feet away, he could see the small, dark holes in the back doors, bullet holes pocking the steel. The attack had come from the rear and the left. Autofire, obviously sound-suppressed, had stitched the length of the driver's side of the vehicle. The shooter, or shooters, had been running as they cut loose. Inside, on the floor, lay three more dead Feds. Their hands were empty. They never got the chance to clear their weapons.

Peering around the van's front bumper, Bolan looked to the end of the cul-de-sac. A floodlit courtyard enclosed by a ten-foot wrought-iron fence stood between him and the safehouse's entrance. There was no sign of movement beyond it. He sprinted down the sidewalk, and finding the tall gate open, he entered. Footprints tracked blood from the porch's steps and down the walk. It was still red.

He had missed whatever happened inside by no more than a few minutes.

The Executioner moved up the stairs to the front doors, which stood slightly ajar. The white-painted, intricately carved wood had been splintered at chest height by a tight group of 9 mm rounds. Easing the door inward, he met with a resilient obstacle. Bolan tried the other door. Inside the foyer, an overweight Hispanic man in a shoulder holster harness lay facedown, his back a gory crater of multiple exit wounds.

Bolan stepped over the corpse's legs. The scale of the safehouse was enormous. A long, high-ceilinged corridor stretched ahead of him. About forty feet away, a second man was down, huddled with his back against the base of the left-hand wall, a stainless steel, 12-gauge riot pump not far from his fingers. Two spent plastic hulls lay by his feet. The Executioner crossed the slick, red-blotched floor, covering the downed man with the Beretta until he got close enough to see that the back of his skull was missing. The contents of the guard's head clung to the thick brushwork of the huge abstract painting on the wall behind him. A graffito of splatter and drip.

The Executioner sensed nothing but death in the mansion, but he had to make sure. Peeking around a corner in the hall, he saw another fallen guard, this one crumpled on the white tile of the vast living room in a pool of his own blood. Bolan grimaced. The bodyguards were bought and paid for by Samosa, as were the Murillos. Why then hadn't the children's protectors cooperated with their fellow employees? From the frontal, all-out nature of the assault, they hadn't been given the chance.

He found the children's bedroom farther along the hall at the rear of the building. The games and toys strewed about the room told him it belonged to young boys. Young rich boys. But what drew his immediate attention was something affixed to the back wall. Bolan stepped closer.

Ramon Murillo was known as "Three Nails" for a reason.

The fourth bodyguard hung suspended by six-inch spikes driven through his open palms and the tops of his bare feet. The nails went through the Sheetrock and deep into the wall studs. Crucifixion hadn't killed him; a shotgun blast to the face had. The spray on the white wall behind his head looked like a gory halo. His blood still dripped, soaking into the carpet.

Bolan searched the room. He found no children's bodies. Nor was there any evidence that they had been harmed in this place. But the boys were gone. Taken.

Suddenly, it all fell into place—why the younger Murillo had killed everyone, why he had left his gruesome calling card. It was his way of driving home a point: Only one thing mattered to the Murillo brothers, that Ortiz kept her mouth shut. All else, even the lives of valued comrades, was trivial. If she gave her evidence to the U.S. government, her kids would die.

The Executioner stared at the abomination on the wall.

What had started out as a simple mission was no longer simple.

In the distance, he could hear a howl of sirens, rapidly growing louder. Someone had phoned in news of the massacre.

It was time to go.

4

Hal Brognola thumbed the remote control, freeze-framing the videotape. The grainy, black-and-white picture on the monitor had been shot through a fish-eye lens that distorted the outer edges of the picture. The central part of the frame, the important part, wasn't affected, however. It showed five men and one woman sitting in the conversation pit of a luxuriously furnished room. A low, glass table separated the facing, sunken couches. On the tabletop were liquor bottles, tumblers, ice bucket, ashtrays and an open attaché case. The date and the time, to the nearest tenth of a second, were burned into the screen's bottom left corner.

One of the men was holding up a thick sheaf of papers he had just taken from the case.

The big Fed zoomed in on the top page and enlarged it. Though the picture quality was too poor for him to actually read the lettering, he recognized the nature of the document from its size, shape and style of decorative engraving.

Bearer bond.

Better than cash.

Untraceable.

Universally negotiable.

Brognola cancelled the VCR's zoom feature and studied each of the slightly blurred faces. He recognized three of the five men on the tape. The Murillo brothers, Roberto and Ramon, and General Augusto Patan of the Mexican army's central command. The pretty woman, frozen in midlaugh, was Yovana Ortiz.

The same Yovana Ortiz who sat across from him in the flesh, nervous and impatient, while he reviewed what she had brought to trade for her life.

"Who are the guys with General Patan?" he asked her.

"Colonel Anibal Montego and Major Jesus Gomez-Herrera. Both officers in the Federal Judicial Police."

Brognola played the tape. It continued to roll for a few more seconds, then blipped off. The brief segment was just a sample, a demonstration copy. A tease.

"Why did you remove the sound track?" he asked.

"You don't need it for verification. What's on that cassette proves I have something valuable to offer the U.S. government, something that will corroborate my eyewitness testimony."

"There's voice on the original?"

"Of course," Ortiz said. "Don't worry, the sound is professional quality, the very best. You can understand every word they say."

Brognola used the remote to shut off the monitor and the VCR. "From what I've seen, I can't tell how much money changed hands here."

"The cash equivalent of 1.5 million U.S."

"Is that specific amount mentioned by these guys?"

"Definitely. The officers argue over how to divide it up. Do we have a deal, then?"

"How many hours are we talking about, total?"

"I went over all of this with the task force...."

"And now you're going to go over it with me. How much tape?"

"I have a hundred hours of unedited footage," she said, "maybe a little more. I videotaped all the money exchanges that took place in my home for seven months."

"How many individuals are involved, and at what levels of government?"

"A dozen high-ranking military officers and federal officials," she said. "Most of them are caught in the act on tape at least twice. It's enough to do exactly what I promised the joint task force: it will break the Samosa cartel's stranglehold on the Mexican government. Do we have a deal?"

The big Fed pushed back in his chair and stretched his arms and legs, letting her question hang in the air. What she was offering sounded too good to be true. Too close to just what the doctor ordered. Though Brognola was the kind of guy who always looked a gift horse in the mouth, suspicious or not, he couldn't walk away from this one. He had to bite. But not before he let her do a little swinging in the wind.

The meeting room was oppressively bleak: unpainted concrete walls and ceiling, gray steel bulkhead doors. They were two hundred feet below ground, in a blastproof, assaultproof bunker. The buried shelter complex and the hilltop mansion above it had been built in Tijuana by a former president of Mexico, though he had never occupied it. The secure nature of their location was a measure of the woman's potential worth to the United States, and of the danger she faced if she really had what she claimed.

With the U.S. President's unreserved private approval, and without the knowledge or consent of the ATF or the FBI, Brognola had taken control of the Murillo-Samosa investigation. Covert and total control. With the help of Mack Bolan, he'd lifted the joint task force's star witness. Yovana Ortiz had vanished in the firefight at the El Zorro Azul club, along with the gunsmoke. None of the FBI or DEA agents in San Diego had a clue what had happened to her.

That was the way it had to be.

There was just too much cartel cash floating around the border, tax-free and up for grabs. One soft spot, one leak, and Yovana Ortiz would be dead, her evidence and the unique opportunity it provided would be lost.

Because of this, Brognola and the President had agreed that the security team protecting her had to be untraceable, way off the books. Which ruled out active U.S. military and federal law enforcement agents. It also had to be incorruptible. The eight men guarding the former Mexican head of state's bunker were all retired Secret Service agents, personally selected by Brognola and the President. They could be trusted to do what had to be done, and to keep their mouths shut. Forever, if necessary.

Even glaring daggers at him, as she was now, Brognola found Ortiz breathtaking. A furious, dark angel. Having researched her thoroughly before this meeting, Brognola knew how she operated. He had come prepared.

Yovana Ortiz was accustomed to using her looks to take exactly what she wanted. A national celebrity, a former beauty queen and television star, she had traveled in Mexico's highest circles of power, mixing with the movers and shakers. She had made the perfect intermediary for the Samosa organization. In a relaxed and friendly atmosphere of upper-crust peers, she was able to bring together the principals charged with keeping drugs out of her country and the drug lord's bribe money.

Brognola asked himself why she had gone along with Samosa's game plan in the first place. After all, she was already living the high life. Why take the terrible risk? It was no secret that the unmarried mother of two had an on-again, off-again romantic relationship with Jorge Luis Samosa. Had she participated in the cartel's business because she loved him? For the excitement? Because she was afraid of him? All of the above?

As part of his prep for this encounter, Brognola had reviewed some of her television work. There was a similarity to her roles on the Mexican soap operas. She always played a self-centered, manipulative, backstabbing bitch. And a very believable, pathological liar. That bothered him, of course. In convincing the joint task force of her bona fides, she had indirectly caused the deaths of six people; for this, she showed no remorse, whatsoever. That bothered him, too.

Apparently, Ortiz was willing to turn on her former lover, but only up to a point. She was ready to bring down all Samosa's Mexican collaborators, but she had steadfastly refused to give a physical description of him.

That bothered Brognola the most of all.

Though the international drug lord had been actively pursued for two decades, no one in law enforcement knew what he looked like. There had never been a photograph or an eyewitness police sketch made of him. Furthermore, no one knew where he was, although it was assumed that he moved freely back and forth between South and Central America.

The U.S. government had already spent hundreds of millions of dollars trying to shut down this faceless, shapeless puppet master. To reach that end, it was prepared to spend hundreds of millions more. Not only was the government serious about bringing him down, it was committed to preventing another drug lord from rising to take his place.

The bulk of the American investment was in training and hardware; most recently, in helping the Mexicans fight the sea war against drugs with a new, integrated, naval-combat technology. In the ebb and flow of this ongoing, low-level conflict, Ortiz's information, if accurate, fit perfectly into the U.S. government's long-range plan. Though it couldn't sink Samosa personally, the destruction of his existing bribery infrastructure would cripple him until the fleet of next-generation, high-speed, drug-interdiction vessels (DIV's) came on-line in Mazatlán. Of course, no matter how state-of-the-art the Mexican drug-fighting ships were, their effectiveness once deployed depended on the incorruptibility of men in the chain of command. Thanks to the woman's video library, the bent military officers could be weeded out long before the first vessel was launched.

In payment for her contribution to the war on drugs, she had asked the joint task force, and now Brognola, for safe transport, new ID, relocation and one hundred thousand dollars a year in spending money in perpetuity. It was a huge expenditure for Witness Protection, but considering what had already been spent on the campaign against the Samosa cartel, her information was a bargain.

"I need to know something more," Brognola told her. His final question went to the base of her credibility. "I need to know why you are doing this. I need to know the truth."

She didn't hesitate a beat. "It's for the sake of my children," she said.

The big Fed studied her face. Though unconfirmed, it had been had been long rumored in the Latin American tabloid press that her sons had been fathered by one of her soap opera costars.

"I know the drug life all too well," she went on. "I know what the drugs do to people and I know what the money does, too. I'm sorry I ever got involved in it. It's never made me happy, only miserable and afraid. I won't let my boys grow up near it. I won't have them polluted by it. I'm doing this for my children, to give them a chance for a real future."

As she spoke, Brognola was looking for "tells," the unconscious gestures, expressions and twitches that sometimes accompany a lie. A furrowed brow, closed eyes, a change in the manner of speech. If she was performing, she deserved an Emmy.

"You didn't have to videotape the money changing hands or agree to give testimony," he said. "You could have just walked away."

"Don Jorge would never have let me leave. He couldn't take the risk. I know too much about how things work and who's involved. The Lord of the Seas doesn't give gold watches to people who want to retire, he gives them coffins.''

A knock on the bulkhead door stopped the conversation. The door opened inward a crack and a stocky middle-aged man with a crew cut, dressed in a white, short-sleeved knit shirt stuck his head in. He carried a CAR-15 on a wide, ballistic nylon shoulder strap. ''Sorry to interrupt you, sir,'' he said. ''But the call you've been waiting for just came in.'' He held out a cellular phone.

''Is it about my children? Are they safe?'' Ortiz asked, as Brognola rose from his chair. ''When will they be here?''

''You'll have to excuse me for a moment,'' he told her, taking the cellular phone and stepping out into the hall. After he'd shut the heavy door behind him, he said, ''Go ahead, Striker.''

Because he was a longtime professional, Brognola's expression didn't change as the Executioner relayed the news. It couldn't have been much worse. Joint task force personnel dead at the scene. All the bodyguards had been slaughtered. The kids were gone, probably in the hands of the Murillos. Without the return of her children, Yovana Ortiz was going to be a problem.

A big problem.

Brognola didn't have to explain the box they were in. He shut up and listened to what the big guy had to say. As always, Bolan's tactical analysis was right on the money. Which was just as well as there was no time for a debate on the course of action. After they had settled the logistics, Brognola said, ''I'll have Grimaldi meet you at the TJ airport, ASAP.'' Then he broke off the connection.

When he reentered the meeting room, Ortiz jumped to her feet. ''Where are my babies?'' she demanded. Show time, Brognola thought. As a father, himself, he sympathized with her situation and her terrible distress, but under the circumstances, any personal feelings had to go out the window. Along with the truth. This woman and her children were stepping-stones to a greater good—the destruction of the Samosa empire. Brognola's job was to take possession of Ortiz's evidence by whatever means necessary and then move on.

"Don't worry, everything's fine," he assured her. "Please, sit, Ms. Ortiz. It's all going exactly according to plan. Can I get you something to eat or drink while you're waiting? Your children are safe and they'll be here with you shortly." His tone of voice was confident, his manner relaxed and easy, as if he believed every word he was saying.

Brognola deserved an Emmy, too.

5

Jack Grimaldi tipped a wing, banking the single-engine Cessna steeply to the east. Through the front windshield, the sunrise over Isla Carmen glowed blood red, Armageddon dawning over the rugged, uninhabited, desert island. Isla Carmen along with its much smaller, northern sister, Isla Coronado, protected the wide bay that fronted the small Baja town of Loreto. As Grimaldi brought the Cessna around, Bolan saw the gasoline lanterns of commercial squid fishermen in their small boats, off the south end of Isla Coronado.

The sky colors changed rapidly, crimson fading to orange, then edging into gold. The surface of the Sea of Cortez shifted from red to vermilion.

"Got enough light now," Grimaldi said into his headset microphone.

"Then let's do it," Bolan told him.

They were six miles south of the Loreto airport.

To touch down at the official, fully paved landing field meant going through a Mexican Customs and Immigration checkpoint. It also meant sitting around most of the morning until the officers in charge managed to drag their butts to work. Neither of which was acceptable. Bolan wanted no record of his arrival and he couldn't afford to lose three or four hours to the Immigration inspector.

Grimaldi continued to bank, easing the Cessna in a wide turn over the smooth-as-glass sea. As he turned, the plane lost altitude and air speed. He leveled out and accelerated, practically skimming the surface of the water with his wheels. Grimaldi glided in over a wide, flat stretch of beach. There were no houses above the high water line, just a flat expanse of scrubland, tinted purple and rose pink. He eased back the power and put the plane down close to the water's edge, where the sand was well-packed. They landed with a hard jolt and, brakes squealing, rapidly slowed to a stop.

The Executioner opened the passenger door, grabbed his backpack and hopped out. Over the engine's roar he said, "See you soon."

Grimaldi grinned and gave him a thumb's-up.

Bolan shut the door and ran around the tail of the plane. As he raced to the crest of the sloping beach, he was buffeted by prop wash and flying sand. The Cessna accelerated away from him. He didn't pause to watch Grimaldi's takeoff, instead, he cut overland, heading for Highway 1.

To the north, the sound of the plane's engine grew fainter and fainter. Takeoff and landing had taken less than three minutes. Bolan jogged on, toward the jagged line of the Sierra de la Giganta mountains in the distance, picking his way around the clumps of brush and piles of rock. There was no fence separating the scrubland from the highway. When he reached the two-lane road, he turned north, toward town, climbing a long, shallow rise. Traffic was nonexistent, but it wasn't quiet. The air seethed with birdsong.

When he reached the summit of the hill, he looked down on an equally long downgrade. Fifty yards away, three olive drab jeeps with canvas tops sat parked on the sand beside the road. A group of soldiers dressed in camo leaned against the trucks, drinking soda pop for breakfast. It was a drug checkpoint. A random inspection station. He saw them and they saw him. It was too late to move off the road now.

As Bolan approached them, he noticed how young they

were. The officer in charge, who had to have been all of twenty, gave him the once-over, then pointedly turned his back. The Executioner was dressed like a tourist. With his backpack and hiking boots, he could have been a European. The place was full of them in the winter, snowbirds from Germany and Austria. One of the soldiers cooked beans and tortillas over a camp stove set up on the tailgate. Nobody stepped into the road and confronted Bolan. The reason: they weren't on duty yet. And they were hungry.

The soldier took note of their weapons in passing. Heckler & Koch assault rifles. The scarred G-3s leaned against the running boards of the trucks. None of them were fitted with magazines. The weapons were all empty. He'd heard the stories about the soldiers having to buy their own bullets, food and diesel for their trucks. No wonder the Murillos could stake out a sanctuary here.

Bolan walked on.

It was another two miles to the outskirts of town. He turned at the soccer field and headed back in the direction of the water. He'd traveled about four blocks past a closed restaurant, a closed beer distributor and a closed grade school when a car pulled up behind him. Bolan turned. It was a police car. The driver followed him for thirty yards, just creeping along, before he swung around in front and stopped, cutting him off.

The driver's door opened and the officer got out. He wore a well-pressed, light-brown uniform. Over the roof of the car said, "How are you doing this morning?"

"I'm good. And you?"

"Things are kind of slow. They usually are this time of day. Your car break down?"

"No, I'm hiking. This is the best time for walking."

The cop agreed. "It'll be way too hot in another couple of hours. You want a ride into town?"

"Sure, why not."

Bolan put his backpack in the rear seat and climbed in.

The police cruiser's dash and headliner had been custom-ized with photos of smiling children.

"Yours?" Bolan asked.

The cop nodded.

"Very beautiful," the Executioner said.

"Where are you going?"

"I need to grab something quick to eat, then I'd like to rent a boat and a captain."

"To do some fishing?"

"Thought I might give it a try."

"I know the perfect place."

They drove down a narrow, cobblestone street, past the weathered, stone facade of a seventeenth century Spanish church. On the tiny central plaza, complete with bandstand, the people of Loreto were starting to show themselves. Men in straw cowboy hats. Women in shapeless cotton dresses. Dogs yapped, roosters crowed.

The officer pulled over to the curb beside a café with small metal tables set out on the sidewalk. The tables were empty, but someone was moving behind the service counter. "Try the *huevos rancheros*," he said. "And as for the fishing boat, tell the cook you want to talk to Jordan. He comes in to eat about this time every day."

"Thanks," Bolan said.

"You're welcome," the cop told him. "I wish I could go fishing."

The Executioner hauled his pack out of the cruiser, then crossed under the café's awning to the service counter. After ordering some food and a cup of coffee, he took a seat out on the sidewalk. In a couple of minutes, other folks started showing up in droves. A few of them were obvi-ously Americans—wearing T-shirts with garish pictures of marlin and tuna on them. Most were locals, and male, in tattered-brimmed, straw cowboy hats and stained long-sleeved shirts.

When the waitress brought him his eggs, he told her he

wanted to talk to Jordan about a boat. She pointed at a red-haired man drinking coffee in the shadows inside. "Jordan," she called.

The man scraped back his folding chair.

One look told Bolan that Jordan was not Mexican. He was freckle-faced, blue-eyed and in the process of growing a prodigious beer gut. Without introducing himself, the man sat at Bolan's table and took out a crumpled pack of Marlboros and lit up. His fingertips were stained orange from nicotine. His once-white, Ohio State T-shirt was now yellow, with an even deeper shade of yellow under the armpits.

"You want to go fishing?" he said in perfect English. "Fishing's been great. You'll have a ball. We've been catching yellowtail, sails, *dorado*. Lots of *cabrilla*, too."

Bolan wiped his mouth with a paper napkin and pushed his plate to one side. "I want a boat and skipper for two days," he said.

"No problem. What hotel are you staying at?"

"I'm not. I want the boat for forty-eight hours. I want to run up the coast toward Mulegé, camp overnight and come back the evening of the second day."

"I can arrange that, but it'll cost you two hundred a day, paid up-front. The captains don't like to stay out all night. They like to sleep in their own beds." Jordan looked at the mostly untouched plate of food. "You done with that? Mind if I..."

Bolan thumbed the plate toward him.

Jordan had his own red plastic fork. He took it out of his T-shirt pocket and started eating. The *huevos rancheros* were gone in the blink of an eye.

Jordan wiped his mouth with the back of his hand and took a pull on his still-burning cigarette. He was a scam artist, and not a very good one. Four hundred bucks was more cash than he'd seen in a month of Sundays. "When can we leave?" the Executioner said.

"I got my truck parked around the corner. We'll swing by Tacho's house, he's the captain, then we'll head down to the marina. Can I carry your bag? It looks heavy."

"No, thanks. I got it."

They piled into the bronze, three-quarter-ton, 1979 Ford. It smelled like an ashtray. There were cigarette butts all over the floorboards. Jordan cranked the Ford, then drove down a maze of sleepy dirt streets before finally pulling into a dusty yard in front of a small house, painted aquamarine. When Jordan got out, Bolan could smell the smoke of wood cooking fires. After he entered the doorless front entrance of the house, there was some loud yelling in Spanish. The red-haired expatriate came back in five minutes with a small, dark-skinned man, who had obviously just been shaken out of bed. They carried plastic bags of food, including oranges, tortillas and beans. And fishing rods.

Jordan made the introductions as they drove toward the water.

"Mucho gusto, señor," Tacho said, offering a callused hand. His front teeth, top and bottom, were capped with stainless steel.

"Same here," Bolan said.

The Loreto marina consisted of a small breakwater with shoreline tie-ups for sports boats. There were no docks. Tacho put the food and soft drinks into the twenty-three-foot Panga's ice chest. Then he and Jordan lugged some thirty-gallon plastic fuel containers from the back of the pickup into the stern of the boat.

"You'll have a great time," Jordan said. He held out his palm, expecting his payment.

Bolan paid him the four hundred, cash. Jordan quickly tucked it away before Tacho could see how much money was changing hands, then he ran full-tilt for his truck.

The soldier sat on the middle thwart seat with his backpack between his feet.

Tacho pull-started the seventy-horse Mariner. Once the

motor was running smoothly, he eased the boat out of the marina.

"Which way?"

"Norte," Bolan told him, *"hacia Punta Pulpito."*

"Okeydoke," Tacho said.

Rounding the breakwater, Tacho opened the throttle. The Panga picked up speed. They ran in close to the beach north of town, angling toward Isla Coronado. Between the mainland and the island was a shallow flat that glowed brilliant turquoise. At its center was a tiny, low-tide island dotted with scraggy-looking cacti. Three pelicans dozed along the shore. Tacho skirted the flat and continued along the coast. To their left the Loreto plain gradually disappeared, replaced by higher and higher shoreline cliffs, until a line of red, desert mountains dropped sheer into the sea.

Small fish jumped along the shoreline rocks, driving sprays of even smaller fish out of the water. To the right, out in the open sea north of Coronado, there was a sudden flurry of activity, splashes, diving birds. Bolan saw four- and five-foot-long fish leaping high in the air.

"Dorado!" Tacho said. "We fish?"

Bolan shook his head. He pointed north.

Tacho shrugged, turning to watch the school of feeding game fish as he steered past.

The Executioner was looking the other way, over the kind of terrain he was going to have to cross and fight in. The mountains were steep. There was no real cover except for the rocks. As the sun was well up, the air temperature had already taken a giant jump. Perspiration was starting to ooze from Bolan's skin, though the speed of the boat helped to cool him off. He took a pair of wraparound sunglasses from his shirt pocket and put them on. The glare off the sea was painful.

They traveled for the better part of two-and-a-half hours along the shore when they came to a shallow, wide bay framed by a series of wind-sculpted, yellow rock formations.

"San Basilio?" Bolan asked.

Tacho nodded.

He pointed to a sandy stretch of shore. "Pull onto the beach over there," he said.

"Okay."

Tacho turned for the beach, slowing the Panga. As they approached the sand, the shimmering heat of the land slammed them. In a smooth motion, the captain cut the outboard and tipped the prop out of the water. The Panga's bow slid up on the sand. "We're here," Tacho said with satisfaction.

"This isn't your boat, is it?" the Executioner said as the skipper walked past him toward the bow.

"No, señor, this boat belongs to the cooperative. I'm just the captain for today."

Bolan stood. "Get out," he said.

"No, I stop for you. Not for me."

The Executioner shook his head. "I want you to get out of the boat, right now."

Something in his passenger's tone of voice, in the look in his cold eyes, made Tacho do exactly as he was told. He hopped barefoot onto the scorching sand.

Bolan found the captain's sneakers on the deck and handed them to him. Then he turned and looted the cooler, giving Tacho back most of the food and drink he'd brought along.

"*Señor,* this is no good," Tacho protested as he set the plastic bags on the beach. "You can't do this."

"It'll take you a full day to walk back to Loreto from here," the soldier told him. "Even if you head due west to the highway and hitchhike from there, it'll still be after dark before you get home."

"Don't leave me here."

"You don't want to go where I'm going, Tacho." Bolan

reached into a pants pocket and took out a thick wad of bills. Without counting them, he slapped the wad into the skipper's hand. "This should help," he said.

Tacho stared in amazement at all the cash in his fist.

"Push me off," Bolan said, stepping to the stern. After the captain had complied, he tilted the motor's lower unit back into the water and gave the pull rope a yank. The Mariner caught on the first try. He backed the Panga away from the beach, then gunned the motor. Bolan looked over his shoulder and saw that Tacho was waving goodbye to him, his metal teeth flashing like tiny mirrors in the sun.

When the Executioner was about a mile off Punta Pulpito, a towering, domed promontory of yellow-brown bedrock that stuck out into the sea, the outboard started to sputter and lose power. The fuel tank was almost empty. He hit the kill switch and the Panga glided to a stop. Before switching the gas line to one of the full tanks, he pulled a sheaf of documents from his backpack. Setting aside the satellite recon map, he tipped up his sunglasses and studied a series of highly detailed, DEA surveillance photos of the coast near the Murillo brothers' ranch.

The shore between Pulpito and Punta Concepción had many protected coves, all quite small and capable of supporting tiny commercial fishing camps, but little more. From the recon documents, he estimated that the cove he sought was a half an hour farther on, in Bahia San Nicolas. After connecting the spare tank and restarting the outboard, Bolan let the motor idle while he found a bottle of water in the cooler. He took a long, slow drink to replace the buckets of sweat that were dripping off of him. Then he pulled down his sunglasses and cranked the Mariner's throttle hard.

6

Carrying a soup bowl-size cup of steaming, black coffee, Roberto Murillo entered his brother's second-floor suite without knocking. He walked across the quarry-tile floor toward a queen-size bed, where Ramon still slept. To reach the bed, Roberto had to pass the suite's hot tub. It was neither bubbling nor steaming. Black glass bottles—Three Generations tequila—floated in it, obviously empty. More evidence of the previous night's fiesta lay on the tile floor beside the hot tub: A gilt-edge mirror, golden razor blade and cocaine in a gallon-size plastic baggy.

Ramon wasn't alone in the bed. Curled up on both sides of him while he snored were a pair of young prostitutes.

Roberto reached down and jerked the covers off. All three were naked.

The girls blinked at him as they struggled to wake up. They made no effort to conceal themselves. They were well trained and well paid. Smiling, they rolled onto their backs, stretched like smooth-skinned cats and parted their thighs.

Roberto ignored them. "Get up, Ramon," he said.

Ramon opened one eye to look at him. "Too early," he said, and closed it. "Come back in four hours."

"We have business."

Ramon stared at the ceiling.

"It won't wait."

With a sudden lurch, the younger Murillo sat up and then jumped off the bed. As he pulled on a pair of baggy slacks, the two women dragged the covers back over themselves and snuggled together in the middle of the bed. Locked in an embrace, they kissed passionately. With tongues.

"Roberto?" Ramon asked, grinning as he shrugged into a black silk shirt.

Roberto said nothing. His brother was the victim of a multitude of vices, including a raging sexual addiction. With access to unlimited funds, Ramon kept a constant flow of beautiful young women cycling through his life. He had a two-a-day habit. This pair would be on the 1 p.m. flight leaving Loreto. The 3 p.m. arriving flight would bring their replacements. Only Ramon wouldn't be here to enjoy them. That was part of the business that wouldn't wait.

When it came to sex, Roberto had more self-control than his brother. It was something he took pride in. Roberto "The Whip" got off in other, equally disturbing ways. He liked power and he liked exercising it. He liked people to be afraid of him and he had given them cause. Virtually no one in Baja was out of his reach. He had proven that time and time again over the past decade.

Roberto also liked the things that unlimited riches could buy. Most of all, he liked being a general with his own private army. He liked planning the big campaign, moving pieces on the game board, doing battle with governments. Ramon was more into the hands-on of the business. Enforcement was his specialty.

Roberto said, "We found the dirty bitch." He handed his brother the cup of coffee.

Ramon sipped, smacked his lips, and said, "She's still in Tijuana, isn't she?"

"How'd you know that?"

"Figured she wouldn't leave her kids behind. Who's got her? The FBI? The DEA? Were they the ones who made the mess of our boys at El Zorro Azul?"

"That's not clear yet. Our informant says that late last night a group of heavily armed men took her to the president's mansion up on the mesa, the one Salinas had built but never lived in.''

''I know that place. I've been inside it. I was actually thinking of buying it once. It's fortified and there are tunnels and an underground bunker system. No way we can drag her out of there. To hunt her down in those tunnels would take an army. Most of our soldiers would die. Yovana is untouchable until she is moved.'' Ramon took another sip of coffee, then said, ''Has the bounty on her head been set yet? How much is Don Jorge willing to pay?''

''Twenty-five million if she dies before she hands over her evidence. Ten million if she dies after she talks to the Feds.''

''We've got to get her to leave the mansion,'' Ramon said. ''If she leaves, she can be hit.''

''The children are the key,'' Roberto told him. ''They're the only thing that will make her show herself.''

''But the FBI or DEA won't let her do that unless they know the boys are safe. We can't give them up to the Feds, Roberto. Don Jorge would go ballistic. He wants his sons back as much as he wants their mother dead.''

''I know, I know, it's a problem. And I'll find a way to deal with it. But you need to fly back to Tijuana this morning and orchestrate the hit on Yovana personally.''

''That will be my pleasure,'' Ramon said. ''Especially if I have a free hand.''

''Do it any way you like,'' Roberto said. ''Just get the job done.''

Ramon put his arm around his brother's shoulder and gave him a quick, manly hug. ''You won't be disappointed,'' he said.

The two Murillos exited the bedroom suite, stepping out into the cool, dark hallway. The facing wall of the corridor was cut out at intervals, forming a series of shaded, second-story balconies that overlooked the pool and gardens.

''The Learjet is already prepped,'' Roberto said as they

started down the staircase. "You can leave at once. I've arranged for a team to meet you at the Tijuana airport when you arrive. They'll have all the particulars, including construction blueprints of the mansion."

"Are Don Jorge's boys awake?"

"They've been up for hours," Roberto said. "They're eating breakfast by the pool."

Ramon beamed at him. "I want to say goodbye to them before I go."

Though the request seemed horrendous under the circumstances, Roberto nodded. Horrendous requests weren't unusual for Ramon. He required a certain amount of humoring in this regard.

A palm-thatched, *palapa* roof shaded part of the white stone deck. The pool was Olympic-size. No one was swimming in it. A half dozen drug soldiers stood around the central fountain wearing communications headsets, carrying stubby, automatic weapons. At a wrought-iron table by the poolside, two children, both blonde and brown-eyed, in striped T-shirts and khaki shorts, sat eating bowls of cornflakes.

"They both look like they've recovered well enough from what happened last night," Ramon said as he and Roberto crossed the patio.

"You shouldn't have let them see—"

"Don't be stupid," Ramon snapped back. "How could I keep them from seeing? I had our men put a blanket over their heads. If they peeked out, what could I do? Besides," he said with a smirk, "such things make a boy into a man. Or have you forgotten?"

"I remember," Roberto said. Then he added, "We were much older."

"Their father will thank me in the end," Ramon told him. "His heirs must be strong if they are to survive."

Roberto knew this was true. He also knew that the boys' father hadn't put any restrictions on what they could do in order to take possession of them. Samosa just wanted them back, alive.

The drug lord wasn't old enough to be the father of either of the Murillos. He could have been an older brother, though; there was a six- or seven-year difference in their ages. Regardless, Roberto looked up to Samosa as a father figure. A man to be respected and feared. A man to obey. The Patron.

As much as Roberto's own lackeys lived in terror of him, he lived in terror of the Lord of the Seas. If the power of money allowed the Murillo brothers to rule Baja, the power of even more money allowed Samosa to rule them. Loyal though the Murillos's soldiers were, none could withstand the hurricane force of Samosa's cash. Given the right amount of money, any of them would turn in an instant. Bodyguard would suddenly become assassin. It was the law of the jungle. Roberto and Ramon had lived by its savage rules for most of their lives.

The two boys looked up from their cereal bowls. Seeing Ramon approaching, they froze. The younger one, Pedro, started to cry. Juanito gave him a hard kick under the table and he stopped at once. Juanito looked up at Ramon and glared.

"How are you boys feeling this morning?" Ramon asked as he pulled up a chair.

Little Pedro was so scared he immediately dropped his spoon. It clattered on the flagstones. Juanito gave him his. "Where is our mama?" the older boy demanded, in a piping, but confident voice.

"Don't be worried about your mama," Ramon said, smiling. "I just got off the telephone with her. She's just fine. She sends you her love. This evening you boys are going to take a boat trip. You'll go to visit your father. Doesn't that sound fun?"

"Where is Mama?" Pedro whined. "Is she coming with us?"

"She'll come later," Ramon said. "Then you'll all be together. You, your mama and your papa. A family again. It'll be great."

This seemed to placate the children, at least temporarily. Perhaps because they wanted so much to believe what Ramon was saying.

Roberto could think of two reasons why Samosa wanted his boys with him. The first had to do with his legacy. Samosa had hacked out an international criminal empire and he wanted to pass it on, to keep control of the drug cartel in the family. To do this, he had to train his young sons to take over the reins. The other reason was even less warm and cuddly. With the boys in his possession, Ortiz would be much less likely to spill the beans. Roberto figured that the Don wouldn't kill his own flesh and blood, unless he had no choice, but he would make damned sure, one way or another, that their mother never saw them again.

"Can we go play on the beach?" Juanito said.

"Are you finished eating?" Roberto asked.

Both boys nodded.

"Then Paolo and the others will drive you down to the beach," Roberto said. He waved over one of the armed guards. "But don't go in the water. There are jellyfish. They'll sting you."

"Can we ride the horses later?" Pedro asked.

"After lunch, if it's not too hot," Roberto said. "Say goodbye to Ramon. He's going back to Tijuana."

"Goodbye," Juanito said, mechanically.

"What about you, little Don?" Ramon demanded of the younger boy. "Cat got your tongue?"

Pedro just stared at him, wide-eyed, unable to speak. His bottom lip started to quiver.

Which made Ramon throw back his head and laugh. He sounded like a mule braying.

Juanito took Pedro by the hand and pulled him away. They followed Paolo around the edge of the pool.

"See how strong they are?" Ramon said. "I didn't damage them. There's nothing to worry about, brother."

It seemed to Roberto that they had plenty to worry about.

The regular flow of under-the-table payoffs were what kept the Murillos's drug-transport route open. Yovana Ortiz was in a position to bring their entire bribery network crashing down. She knew all the names; she had made most of the payoffs.

And that was the least of their problems.

If every one of the officials currently on the Murillo/Samosa payroll got busted, it wouldn't be the end of the world. In time, new officials could be corrupted and the system reinstated. Other problems loomed on the horizon, bigger problems, in the form of the joint Mexican-U.S. drug-interdiction vessel, known as the DIV program. The program's funding was a matter of public record in both countries. The technical details and the names of the major contractors had been widely reported in the international press. The U.S. government wanted the cartel to know what was coming, and to rub its nose in it.

These new generation DIVs combined satellite target acquisition, high-speed pursuit and fully automated weapons systems, including ground-to-ground and ground-to-air missiles. On paper, at least, the proposed fleet had the power to destroy what it had taken Jorge Luis Samosa and the Murillos decades to put together. A handful of these special attack ships patrolling in key areas would squeeze off the flow of product between Central and South America and the U.S. in a stranglehold; the losses would quickly add up. In order to maintain its vast cash flow and the loyalty of its thousands of employees, the Samosa organization moved drugs in mass quantities. In that regard, the cartel was like a runaway train. Unless Samosa could find another high-capacity route, ultimately the DIVs would drive him out of business and, by domino effect, the Murillos as well.

That crisis needed to be dealt with well in advance, before the launch of the first ship. Roberto firmly believed that there was no hole that couldn't be stopped up with money, when applied in sufficient quantity. Quantity was never an issue, as demonstrated by the staggering price Samosa had placed on Yovana Ortiz's head. For the Murillo brothers, that huge bounty meant next to nothing. What mattered was the sword Ortiz held over their livelihood. Such a betrayal demanded payback.

As Ramon turned to go, Roberto told him, "Just make sure you erase the bitch."

"With pleasure."

7

Because the mouth of the small cove known as San Bartolomeo was protected on its southern side by a curve of solid rock, even with the DEA photographs, Mack Bolan might have missed the entrance had he not been running so close to shore. He steered around the end of the wave-lapped, rock spit and into the cove.

Over unknown centuries, a seasonal stream had carved a narrow canyon out of the seventy-five-foot high volcanic plain. He scanned the rimrock and saw a number of possible sniper hideouts. There were also piles of huge rock blocks that didn't look at all natural. They looked like they had been pushed into place by a bulldozer. Probably gun positions, he thought, which could make getting in or getting out of the cove almost impossible.

Something flashed at him from the rim. A single bright wink as the sun reflected off the front lens of a telescopic sight. At least one of the sniper positions was occupied. Retreat was out of the question. The shooter had him dead to rights.

Bolan slowed the Panga to a crawl, turning his attention to the other boats moored to floats in the middle of the tiny bay. Neither the satellite view from space, nor the weeks-old, side-scanning photos taken by DEA aircraft could tell him what condition the craft were in. He had to judge that for himself. The Executioner wasn't counting on having to make an escape by water in a commandeered boat, but as he knew all too well, when the numbers started falling the best laid plans could change in a heartbeat.

Beached on the gravel at the end of the cove were a pair of Pangas with seventy-five-horse outboards. He couldn't see any tall, portable fuel tanks inside either boat. Which meant he couldn't count on making it back to Loreto in one. He couldn't count on making it out of the back of the cove, either. The far end was a definite death trap.

Once the site of a fish camp, San Bartolomeo was now part of the Murillos's desert rancho. The open-sided, *palapa*-roofed, fishermen's shacks that had once dotted the cove's shore had been torn down. They had been replaced with little houses; permanent dwellings built on concrete pads above the high waterline. Most looked shut up, unoccupied.

Most, but not all.

A white-bearded guy in a frazzle-brimmed straw cowboy hat waved at him from the shade of his porch. He sat on a lawn chair beside his trailer, drinking something out of a big, insulated mug.

Bolan waved back. As the Executioner approached the gravel beach, he reached down and flipped the motor lock. He gunned the engine to get a tad more speed, then shut it off as the Panga slid up onto the beach.

Right away, the white-bearded man got up from his lawn chair and started walking around the curve of the beach toward him. Three other guys came out of their houses and did the same. They seemed in no particular hurry. All of them looked like American expatriates. None carried visible weapons.

From somewhere out of sight on the plain above, a plane took off. A jet plane. It didn't pass overhead and the engine's shrill scream grew rapidly fainter.

Bolan jumped out of the bow and tied the Panga to the line the other boats were tethered to.

The white-bearded guy crunched over the gravel in his

flip-flops. He carried two thermos mugs. He set one down on a big rock and extended his hand to the stranger.

"Morning," he said. "I'm Frank Chip, you got some engine trouble?"

"Name's Mike Belasko," Bolan said shaking the man's hand. "Got no trouble. I was just running up the coast and I thought I'd stop and have a look at your cove."

"Good thing your power's okay, cause this is an outboard graveyard. Nobody here can fix them. Oh, the Mexicans can take them apart all right. But that's the way they stay."

Chip glanced at the knife sheathed at Bolan's waist. It was a SOG SEAL-2000, 12 1/4 inches of stainless steel. "Hell of a blade you're carrying there."

"It does the job," the Executioner said.

Though the tattoo on Chip's forearm was blurred with age and scars, Bolan could still read it: Death from Above.

The other men wandered down to the shore and joined them. They were all younger than Chip, in their midforties and deeply suntanned. These weren't the kind of drug soldiers Bolan had come up against in Tijuana. They weren't "organization men," not by any stretch of the imagination.

Chip introduced the black-bearded guy with skinny legs as Ryan, the man in a crusty, brown felt cowboy hat as Edwards, and the fourth man with the big, soft beer belly as Carlson. Carlson had come down from the largest house on the cove. Like his pals, he carried a thermos mug in one hand. In the other, he had a plastic jug with a clear liquid in it. The outside of the jug was frosty, as if it had just been taken out of a freezer.

Bolan noticed the way these guys backed away from him after shaking hands, making sure the sniper on the rim had a clear angle and that they were out of the line of fire. When the Executioner moved toward them, they shifted to the side.

Cute.

"You get the Panga from Arturo's?" Edwards asked, looking at the name "Suzi" crudely painted on the bow.

"Jordan got it for me," Bolan replied.

"He rented it to you without a skipper? He never does that."

"I paid extra."

"Must've cost a bundle." Edwards said as he walked to the stern of the Panga, staring hard at the black ballistic nylon duffel bag that sat next to the auxiliary gas tank. There was no way he could tell what was inside, not without opening it.

"I don't like to feel crowded," Bolan said. "And I like to do my own navigating."

"Where are you headed?" Carlson asked.

"Got no definite plans. I'm just poking around the coast. Nice and isolated around here. Really peaceful. I'll be camping on the beach on the way up to Mulegé." He indicated the marooned captain's gear leaning against the edge of the bow platform. "Maybe I'll stop and fish. I have to turn around and come back in few days. Got a flight back to L.A. in a week."

"Thirsty?" Chip said.

Bolan accepted the mug the man offered him. He took a sip from it. The liquid was ice-cold but it burned like fire going down. It smelled and tasted like fuel oil mixed with industrial solvent. It was straight tequila of the very cheapest sort. The Executioner glanced at the label on Carlson's half-frozen jug: Oso Negro. He pretended to take another drink while the others tipped their mugs way back.

He didn't have to ask these guys what they did here.

They were doing it.

They weren't hired muscle, they were a smoke screen. An early warning system in case some other drug dealers, or the Mexican marines or federal judicial police tried to assault the site from the sea. They didn't have to fight. All they had to do was occupy the invaders with their drunken gringo routine. They worked as a team with the sniper on the rim, distracting potential targets until the shooter had them zeroed in.

"You guys got a real sweet setup here," Bolan said. "Your own private cove. Do you own those houses?"

Chip shook his head. "The owners of the rancho up on the plain rent the land to us. They let us build houses on it."

"You got power?"

"Off-the-grid," Ryan said. "Solar panels and gas-powered generators. The refrigerators are all propane."

"Sounds ideal. What about the other houses?"

"Some folks come down here a couple weeks a year," Chip said. "The rest of the time they keep their places shut up."

A little yellow dog crossed the beach and came toward them. It was solidly built; its ears and shoulders deeply scarred. It didn't bark, didn't wag its curly tail. It just watched intently. "Your dog?" Bolan said.

"That's nobody's dog," Ryan said. "He comes over from San Nicolas a couple times a week. Doesn't have a name. Hangs out here for scraps. Because Edwards started feeding him."

"He's a good dog," Edwards said. "Kills snakes."

"Want a top-up?" Carlson asked.

"No, I'm fine," Bolan said. "Got a long way to go this morning. Tequila and sun give me a headache. Especially before 10 a.m."

Either it didn't give these expats a headache, or they didn't care. Carlson topped up the mugs.

In silence, the soldier watched them power down the Oso Negro. He recognized the breed. They reminded him of men who had stayed behind in Vietnam after their discharges, or who had gone back to Southeast Asia after a few months in the States. Men bit bad by the third world bug. In the world's less-traveled places it was still like the

Wild West. The anything-goes mentality was hard to shake. In certain men, a limitless playing field tended to bring out the scumball in a large way. Sex. Booze. Drugs. Murder.

A bicycle with two riders appeared from out of the palm trees up the canyon. A small Mexican man was steering erratically, in part, no doubt, due to the large woman sitting on the handlebars.

"It's Cipriano and his niece," Carlson said. He hurriedly stashed the icy jug behind a boulder.

When the bike's front wheel hit the gravel, the man lost control and crashed, dumping the woman and himself onto the beach. The driver had salt-and-pepper stubble on his cheeks and one glass eye. The white of his real eye was yellow and bloodshot. He was so drunk that he couldn't stand without leaning against the side of the beached Panga. He spoke in a deep, gravelly baritone. "You got a drink for Cipriano?"

"No, we don't," Carlson said. "Fuck off."

His niece was wearing a flannel shirt over a cotton dress and red wool socks in unlaced high-top sneakers. Her greasy hair was parted in the middle and plastered to the sides of her head. She looked demented.

Cipriano hooked a thumb at the woman. "You can have her for a pint," he said.

There were no takers among the expatriates.

"A half-pint, then."

Still no takers.

"A half-pint and all of you can have her."

The girl tittered into her hand. Clearly, she wasn't opposed to the transaction.

"Jesus," Chip said to Carlson, "just give the bastard a drink and make him go away."

Beaming triumphantly, Cipriano produced a dented metal cup. Carlson filled it halfway with cold tequila. The Mexican drank a deep swallow, then held out his cup again.

When nothing more was offered, he tapped the rim impatiently with a grimy forefinger.

"Nah, that's it, man," Carlson said, waving him off. "That's all you get. Beat it."

Cipriano shrugged. Then he growled something at the girl. As he turned back for the palm trees, she picked up the bike and started walking it up the track after him.

Bolan didn't ask who the guy was because he didn't care. But Chip told him, anyway.

"Cipriano used to be the ranch foreman here," he said. "Until the Oso Negro melted his brain. He got so drunk one time that he fell out of a palm tree and hit his head. That's how he lost his eye. The patrons let him stay on, even though he's useless for work. Guess he was pretty useless before, anyway. He claims the girl is his niece, but she isn't. They live in a shack up in the palm grove. The girl cooks for him, washes his clothes, whores for him, whatever he wants. There ain't enough tequila in Baja to make me go near that one."

The other expats grunted in agreement. Then they sipped their drinks.

"Do you guys hang out with the owners of the rancho?"

His question hung in the air, which had suddenly turned frosty, despite the heat. The Executioner had poked a tender area.

"I just wondered who they were."

"Rich Mexicans," Chip said, curtly. "They don't ever come down here, except to use their yacht, which is moored someplace else right now. Down at Cabo San Lucas, I think. They spend most of their time away from the rancho. Got businesses in the States."

"You got a sweet deal," Bolan said again.

From the palm grove came the growl of an engine. After a few seconds a black Jeep CJ5 appeared. Because the top was off, the Executioner could see all the occupants. Two big Mexican men sat in front, one in back with two small children.

"More company," Bolan said.

"It's Paolo," Edwards said.

"And who might that be?"

"Head of rancho security," Chip replied.

"Whose kids?" the Executioner asked. He already knew the answer to that one.

"Maybe you'd better shove off now," Chip told him. "The patrons don't much like people landing boats in their cove without permission."

The Jeep stopped momentarily on the other side of the high-water mark. Two of the men hopped out and moved purposefully toward him. They were dressed in sports shirts and slacks. The shirts were open to the waist, displaying their collections of gold chains and their huge, bulked-up pecs. The short sleeves of their shirts were rolled up to better show off massive biceps. On their hips, they wore holstered, big-frame semiautomatic weapons.

The guy in front pulled his pistol and, making sure Bolan saw him, dropped the safety. "You got ten seconds to get in that Panga and beat it," he said as he stepped up. He raised the pistol and took aim. "Otherwise, I'm going to shoot you in the head."

The other drug thug drew his weapon, as well.

Behind them, the Jeep's driver put it in gear, taking the kids along the track that bordered the beach, heading for the mouth of the cove.

"I wouldn't want that to happen," the Executioner said. As he spoke, he backed up with his hands in the air. He knelt and quickly untied the tether, then shoved the Panga off the beach and hopped in.

Murillos's security men and the expats watched him pull-start the outboard. As he turned for the open sea, Bolan smiled and waved at them.

He'd see them again soon.

Juanito and Pedro watched from the back seat of the Jeep as Paolo and the other guard drew their pistols and aimed them at the tall stranger. Though they were accustomed to seeing firearms and being surrounded by a forest of security men, the events of the previous night had forever altered their perception of what guns could do.

"Is he bad?" Pedro asked.

"I don't know."

"Are they going to shoot him now?"

Juanito was getting very nervous remembering the sight of the dead people, the dead people who had taken care of him, their blood splashed everywhere. There was no one to comfort or help him, now. He had to be a big boy.

"Are they?" Pedro repeated, insistently.

"How should I know?" he snapped back at his brother.

"I'm scared, Juanito."

"Don't be such a baby."

The driver pulled away from the standoff and sped down the narrow lane that ran along the bottom of the cliff. Yovana Ortiz's sons turned their heads, watching the tall man and the guns, expecting, dreading the hard crack of a pistol shot. It didn't happen. They saw the stranger push his boat off the beach and jump in.

Juanito was relieved.

When the driver stopped the Jeep, Juanito jumped out and scrambled down the loose rocks to the water. Right away, he found a stick to play with, just the right length for a sword or machete. Pedro got himself one, too.

When the stranger's outboard motor started up, both boys flinched.

Pedro dropped his stick and started to cry. "Where's Mama?" he said. "Did they hurt our mama, too?"

"Mama's coming soon," Juanito told him. He didn't know if he believed it, though. "And we're all going to go visit Papa."

"I love Papa."

Juanito loved him, too. They didn't get to see him much, even when they were living at his house. Their father was always busy. Always going somewhere in a hurry. But when he was around, he was the most fun to play with. Better than their mother or any of the bodyguards. Their father knew how to get his sons real excited, how to tickle their imaginations. He treated them really well—not just giving them anything they wanted, but giving them what they needed. They had a sense of complete safety when they were around him. Juanito knew their father was the strongest man in the world. And the bravest.

Not even his biggest bodyguard would look him in the eye. When he spoke, his men always looked at their shoes. Even their uncles, who weren't really uncles, Roberto and Ramon, did this.

At his house in Panama, their father had once killed a big red-and-black snake in the shower stall. It had crawled in through the bathroom window. He killed it in front of his boys with a machete. He showed them how to do it. He first used the flat side of the blade against the side of the snake's head. Then he chopped off the head in one swing. The snake's body had thrashed around in the shower, spurting blood. When it was dead, they measured it. It was eight feet long.

Their father had then put the machete into Juanito's hand and told him, "Next time you will do it, son."

Juanito grabbed hold of a strand of bull kelp and struggled to drag it free of the heap. "Come on, help me pull this out," he told Pedro. The two boys were tugging away on the heavy length of kelp as the stranger drove past in his Panga, heading north. Their driver watched the man until his boat was out of sight.

Once they had the strand of kelp pulled loose, Juanito and Pedro played one of their favorite games.

"Look out for the snake!" Pedro shrieked.

Eyes narrowed, Juanito lined up his strike. He whacked the bulb end with his stick just as he had the headless body of the snake in the shower stall. With his father shouting encouragement, he had struck it harder and harder, until the machete had severed the backbone.

Juanito's father had dipped a finger in the snake's blood, then wiped it on Juanito's face, a single red smear down his chin.

"Good boy," his father had said, mussing his hair.

In his mind, Juanito could hear those words as he furiously beat the kelp. Pedro had recovered his own stick and was mimicking his big brother, attacking the other end of the pretend snake.

They pounded it until it was broken in a dozen places, then they stopped to catch their breaths.

Another car drove out from under the palm trees. It stopped on the edge of the gravel. The driver and his passenger got out. They helped Paolo and the other man drag the rancho's Radon boat over to the beach. Paolo and two of the men climbed in and started the boat's motor. They headed out of the cove at high speed, throwing such a big wave up on the shore that the boys had to back up or get drenched.

Then their driver's walkie-talkie crackled. He held it up to his ear and listened. When he lowered it, he said, "We have to go back to the rancho now. Get in the car. Quickly."

The boys didn't want to leave the beach so soon, but they didn't protest. From the man's stern tone of voice, they knew it wouldn't do any good.

A little farther on, the driver turned at a fork in the road and lumbered up the grade to the top of the plateau. At the summit was a gate made of bright steel. The fence that enclosed the rancho was steel, too, with steel fence posts. A long, skinny house with a palm-roof porch stood beside the gate. Two guards with machine guns stepped out of the shade. They waved the Jeep on.

Rancho Murillo sat in the middle of the barren, sun-blasted, volcanic plain, surrounded by a high wall of white-plastered mud bricks. The sprawling rancho was two stories tall and coated with mud-colored adobe, as were the outbuildings, storage sheds and bunkhouses.

Neither Juanito nor Pedro liked the rancho very much. According to Roberto and Ramon, the Baja was chock-full of bad things that small boys could get into. Things like scorpions, tarantulas, rattlers and clouds of wasps. Because of this, their uncles placed severe limitations on what the boys could do and where they could do it. They had to be under constant watch when they were outside. They had to wear hard shoes, too. Neither boy was afraid of the desert, but neither had been stung, yet.

"When are we going to see Mama?" Pedro asked as they drove through the gap in the picturesque wall.

"Later," Juanito answered. "We'll see her later."

"What if she doesn't come?"

"Shut up."

9

The Executioner glanced over his shoulder and saw the blue Radon boat following about five hundred yards back. Even at that distance, he could make out three heads behind the windshield. That he was being pursued didn't surprise him He figured he had to have made a real impression on the inhabitants of San Bartolomeo.

A bad one.

Why hadn't they killed him, then? Why had they let him get back in his boat and gun away?

Bolan asked himself those questions as he twisted the throttle handle until it would turn no more. Though the engine noise got much louder, there was no accompanying increase in speed. The outboard was maxed out. He steered closer to the rugged shoreline, sticking to the smooth water where he could make the most speed.

When he looked over his shoulder again, the Radon was slowly gaining on him, which puzzled him for a second. The other boat had a lot more power than his Panga. Even carrying three men, it could've overrun him easily. So, the Radon's driver was hanging back on purpose, letting him put some distance between himself and the cove. In the direction he was headed, there was nothing but mile after mile of deserted beach. The men in the Radon didn't want anyone to see what they were going to do to him.

He tested his theory by abruptly slowing his pace. The

Radon slowed even more. Theory validated, he cranked the Mariner back to the max.

The soldier guessed they had already chosen a specific killzone. Someplace they had used successfully before. He had a certain landing spot in mind, too. He had picked it out after a detailed search of the satellite map and DEA photos. As he skirted the coastline, he was looking for a particular rock formation, a place where a jutting promontory of bedrock had been eroded into the sea. The tumbled, massive blocks of lava choked a small bay, creating a narrow, zigzagging channel that led to the shore.

When he came upon the rock-choked bay, he started searching for a specific landmark, two stone monoliths tipped end to end, like the peak of a roof. When he found it, he dropped his speed again and headed sharply toward shore. This time the other boat accelerated, swinging wide to the north to cut him off.

Maybe they had the same spot in mind?

Bolan ran straight into the passage. The tide level was just right—the tops of the fallen blocks that formed the channel were ten feet above the water. As he turned out of sight around the first corner, the passage narrowed quickly. Jumbled blocks formed an obstacle course. Traversing it, he scraped the sides and bottom of the Panga's hull. Clearing the next bend, he immediately cut his engine. The fit was too tight for him to turn the boat. He didn't care. He wasn't going any farther in the Panga. Ahead, there were more rocks than water, a series of landlocked pools between him and the shore. The mainland rose in a steeply sloping hill sparsely dotted with brush and cacti.

He took off his sunglasses and set them on the seat. Then he opened the duffel bag and pulled out his suppressor-equipped Ingram submachine gun and the fully loaded combat harness. As he shrugged into the harness, he could hear the other boat approaching the channel entrance. The engine noise fell off as it slowed to a crawl. Picking up the

MAC-10, Bolan jumped out of the Panga and onto the face of a tilted boulder. He scrambled over the top and down the back, then he rock-hopped around the channel, using the cover of the boulders to return unseen to the entrance. Because there were so many big blocks, it was easy going and he moved quickly and quietly. When he reached the mouth of the passage, he stopped and clung to a stone slab. After a minute or two, the sound of the Radon's idling motor grew louder and he could hear his pursuers talking in rapid-fire Spanish.

The Radon's hull shrieked against the near wall of the channel.

"This way!" one of the men said.

The boat's engine revved hard as the driver tried to correct his course.

Digging the toes of his shoes into the stone, Bolan prepared to strike.

PAOLO GROWLED a curse and pushed the Radon's shift lever forward. Too far. The boat lurched ahead, slamming into the opposite wall. Enrique did a frantic little two-step to keep from being dumped overboard. Paolo felt rage building within him, a terrible outward pressure inside his chest and skull. He wanted to pound the throttle down with his fist and ram his way into the passage. Either that, or jump in the water, pick up the damned boat and throw it onto the shore.

Paolo had just finished a course of "the juice"—anabolic steroids taken to stimulate rapid muscle growth—and he was feeling strong. Invincible, in fact. The bulk-up drugs always had that effect on him. But he wasn't totally insane. Instead of trying to shot-put the Radon, he shifted into reverse, the clutch chattering before the transmission caught. As soon as they were moving backward, he shifted forward again. The Radon slipped past the sheer wall, gliding deeper into the channel.

Intent over the sights of their M-16s, Enrique, in the bow, and Juan, who stood by Paolo's side, swept the terrain on all sides. They all knew that the tall stranger couldn't have run far. He didn't have time. The game of cat and mouse would soon be over, Paolo thought. And the cat would have its dinner.

The Murillos weren't taking any chances with trespassers. Not after what had happened at their Tijuana nightclub. And not with hostages as valuable as Samosa's kids staying at the rancho. Paolo would've gladly done the guy right there on the beach, but his orders from Roberto Murillo had been emphatic: There was to be no more killing in front of the children, unless it was absolutely necessary.

Paolo grinned. Things always seemed to work out for the best.

As he'd climbed into the Radon, the Anglo guards had warned him that the tall stranger was possible big trouble. But Paolo had looked the man in the eyes. The tall one didn't know what trouble was. Until now.

The excess of confidence that the Murillos's head of security felt wasn't only due to the drugs circulating in his bloodstream. He knew the odds were three to one in his favor. He knew he and his men had automatic weapons and they had done the same kind of job in this very spot several times before.

Nobody was going to come to save this gringo.

The only sound in the channel came from the Radon's engine, a soft idle as it pushed the boat forward dead slow. Paolo put his lips together and started making kissing noises.

Enrique looked back, grimacing. He shook his head. Paolo was giving away their position.

Juan, who had also just done a course of the steroids, laughed out loud, then followed Paolo's lead.

Paolo picked up the Uzi from the dash and held it in his right hand, steering the Radon with his left. "Hey, man," he crooned to the surrounding rocks, "we're going to fuck you up."

THE EXECUTIONER ignored the catcalls and concentrated on the engine sound. He knew that as the Radon approached the first turn, the driver would have both hands full maneuvering around it. The turn was tight, and the channel beyond it narrowed even more. The two gunmen would be thinking about what was just around the corner. Not what was directly behind them.

When the motor sound dropped, Bolan pushed up, raising his head above the top of the rock slab. The scene below was almost exactly as he had visualized it. There were two guys behind the boat's windshield, the driver at the helm and another gunner standing on the gunwale with an M-16. The gunner held his autorifle aimed directly ahead. The third man was standing on the bow. He, too, was ready to shoot at anything that appeared around the corner in front of them. For an instant, their rear was undefended.

An instant was all it took.

The Executioner opened fire at once and without warning. The MAC-10's bolt clattered maniacally as its muzzle spit hollowpoint slugs. The hardman on the gunwale twisted sideways, arms flying limp and wide, his M-16 cartwheeling away. Trigger pinned, Bolan walked a line of fire up over the dashboard, through the windshield's glass and into the man perched on the bow. Slammed backward to the very edge of the bow's deck, he dropped to his hands and knees, then slumped to his face.

The captain had grabbed a machine pistol from the dashboard in front of him. Before he could swivel and bring it to bear, Bolan caught him midchest with a half dozen 9 mm slugs. Momentarily pinned by the impacts, his back against the wheel, he pitched forward, crashing to the deck, where he flopped and twisted.

No more kissing sounds came from his lips, only a high, shrill mewling.

The cloud of cordite smoke that surrounded Bolan drifted slowly away, out to sea. As he dumped the spent magazine and slapped home a fresh one, his eyes never left the kill-zone. Pilotless, the Radon inched forward until its bow rammed the wall of rock directly ahead. Nobody on the boat tried to get up. After a few seconds, the moaning stopped and all three lay very still.

The Executioner removed his shoes and socks, then stripped out of his harness. The MAC-10 he left on the rock as well. Drawing his SEAL-2000 knife, he jumped from the rock to the bow. The fallen man's blood oozed over the deck and drooled off the sides. A goner.

Bolan quickly scrambled around the cuddy and checked the other two. They were likewise dead; the decks sheeted with their blood. Resheathing his blade, he moved to the stern. He took the helm and, with a grinding jerk, dropped the Radon into reverse. He backed all the way out of the rocky channel. The Executioner turned away from land, watching the depth sounder on the dashboard. When the bottom dropped to sixty feet, he shifted to neutral and checked the wind's direction. There was none to speak of. And very little drift from current. He shut off the motor.

Leaning over the edge of the hold, Bolan reached down and opened the bilge drains. Two inch-thick jets of sea-water squirted in. Then he grabbed the driver by the wrist and dragged him to the foot of the compartment. Lifting him by the trouser waistband at the small of his back, Bolan dumped him headfirst into the engine hold. He did the same with the other two.

By the time the last body went in, seawater was already swirling up around the motor's valve covers. The dead men's arms floated above their heads, hands waving limply in the flow. Bolan closed the hatch far enough to hook the latch, but didn't batten it down. Thus hooked, the latch held the hatch open about an inch on its bow-facing side. An all-important inch.

The Executioner opened the door to the cuddy. He retrieved the M-16 from the bow, aimed it through the open doorway and emptied the full magazine, thirty rounds, into the hull. Fiberglass splinters swirled in gunsmoke, whooshing out the cabin entrance, making him squint. When the smoke cleared he saw the water rushing in. Almost at once, the bow started to tip down.

He waited until the sea was ankle deep on the deck and washing away the already clotting blood, then he dived off the gunwale. The water was warm and very salty. It made for easy swimming. As he stroked for shore, the air trapped in the engine compartment shot out through the gap in the hatch. And the Radon went down with an explosive hiss.

He swam on without looking back. He climbed out and surveyed the scene. There was no trace of the Radon. No floating bodies. Not even an oilslick. If the Murillos sent more troops out searching, they would find nothing here.

That was the only bright side.

The last thing Bolan had wanted was to show his hand this early in the day. His plan had been to arrive at the rancho at sunset and use the failing light to make his entry and escape. Now he couldn't afford to wait that long. When the Radon crew didn't return in a couple of hours, the red flags were going to go up, and the rancho would go on full alert. Worst-case scenario: The Murillos could fly the kids out. That was something he couldn't allow to happen.

The broiling sun dried his feet in a hurry. He donned his socks and shoes and, lugging his harness and weapon, picked his way back to the Panga. The first thing he did was put on the polarized sunglasses so he could see into the water. He started the motor and eased the boat deeper into the rocky maze. When he could go no farther, when the bow crunched solidly into a barely submerged boulder, he shut off the engine. The air closer to land was at least fifteen degrees hotter.

He opened the duffel and took what he needed. A full daylight raid called for desert camouflage fatigues and boots, and nonreflective face makeup. After changing clothes, he put together the M-89 sniper rifle, attached the Leupold Ultra M-3 scope and the custom-made Arconus suppressor. Scope, barrel and stock were already wrapped with nonreflective brown tape. He checked the 10-round magazine to make sure it was full, then set out the remainder of his gear. With the Ingram submachine gun, the long gun, the Beretta 93-R, extra ammo, the loaded harness and a water bottle, he was carrying close to eighty pounds.

The soldier hopped rocks until he hit the narrow beach. Before he started up the hill, he checked his watch for the start time. As he ascended, sand quickly gave way to light-brown dirt and jagged rocks. Vegetation dwindled. Sweat peeled down the sides of his face, but there was no breeze to cool him off.

By the time he got to the top of the ridge, his fresh shirt was soaked through and the volcanic rock had turned his new boots into old ones. He took a swig of water. Bugs he couldn't see were singing in the shimmering, dizzying heat. The sea below was like glass.

People didn't walk this stretch of coast. They drove by it in boats. Paddled past it in kayaks. It was too hot. There was way too much up and down, steep rises, sheer drops. There was no fresh water. Break a leg or twist an ankle in this locale and you'd be buzzard food in two days.

The prevailing opinion was that no one in their right mind would try to hike it.

That was an assumption Bolan was counting on. He was staking his life on it.

Though the heat grew much more intense the farther he got from the shore, he had to go inland, breaking his own trail through the desert. He followed the line of least resistance. Better to scale the steep hills than to waste time and energy rock climbing the nearshore.

Sweat inside his shoes soaked his socks. They squished with every step.

HE'D BEEN WALKING south for an hour when he caught sight of a second boat, a Panga racing up the coast at high speed.

Bolan moved downslope, well below the crest of the hill, and hunkered there on one knee. He didn't want to get caught silhouetted against the cloudless sky. He didn't unsling the long gun to use its telescopic sight, since a flash could give him away.

He knelt there, sweating, while he watched the boat run toward him. It could have just been a commercial fisherman looking to work the inshore reefs in the area.

It wasn't.

When the Panga was directly across from and below him, he could see the four guys riding in it. They weren't dressed like fishermen, commercial or otherwise. As a rule, fishermen didn't wear shoulder holsters. They didn't carry assault rifles, either.

Obviously, the soldiers in the Radon had already been missed. He recalled that there had been a VHF radio on board. Maybe someone at the rancho had tried to reach them. Tried and failed. It was difficult to reach dead men at the bottom of the sea. The follow-up Panga might run all the way to Mulegé, another fifteen miles, before its occupants decided something wasn't right and turned back.

By that time, the show would be over, one way or another.

Bolan waited until the search party had passed by, then he rose from his crouch and started running.

10

Hal Brognola descended the long flight of stairs carrying a cardboard tray of food and soft drinks. What a depressing place, he thought. Concrete tunnel walls without paint, concrete floor gritty under the leather soles of his shoes. Bare lightbulbs in the ceiling. Standing water in the corners. One expected something more, even in the way of a bunker, from a multimillionaire head of state.

Above the grim subterranean corridors, the sun had come up long ago. It had been almost four hours since Jack Grimaldi had last reported in, and then just to confirm that Bolan had been dropped off on the beach south of Loreto.

The trouble had started before then.

A couple of hours after Bolan had failed to show up with her children, Yovana Ortiz had forced Brognola to tell her what had really happened. There just hadn't been any way around it. There was no wiggle room left for him. She had made a terrible scene when she learned that her kids weren't in U.S. custody or under the protection of her own bodyguards, but rather, in the hands of the Murillo brothers. If she hadn't been physically restrained by two of the Secret Service men, she would have clawed the big Fed's eyes out.

Brognola was an honorable man, a man who held himself to a higher standard, but he was also a good soldier. He did what had to be done to accomplish the mission. Even if that meant catching some backlash or getting his face raked by fingernails.

Brognola had let her stew over her predicament in isolation. During the first few minutes of that two-hour timeout, Ortiz had destroyed the video monitor and tape deck with a handy chair. Now it was time to reestablish contact. He hoped she'd exhausted herself. In case she hadn't, a Secret Service man entered the room with him.

They found the woman sitting quietly, her face tearstained, her mascara smeared, but her attitude adjusted.

What choice did she have, after all, but to go along with the program?

She was essentially a prisoner surrounded by armed guards in a cell deep underground. Even if she were free, her children would be lost to her. There was no way she could get them back by herself. And if she somehow did manage to get them back, how long would she last before the Murillos's hitmen found her and finished the job? Her only hope for her and her children was Brognola and what he had to offer.

She knew that, now. She had accepted it. He could see that in her defeated eyes.

"Is there any word, yet?" she asked.

"Nothing new."

"Where did they take my boys?"

"The ranch at San Bartolomeo," he said. "Our extraction team is in position by now. I expect to hear from them in the next two hours, but only after the mission is completed."

"Your man, the one with the cold eyes?"

"Yes?"

"He's in charge?"

"Yes. If anyone can do the job, he can."

"I've been to the rancho," she said. "It is a fortress. There are many drug soldiers there. They won't hesitate to kill. If the Murillos realize they are under attack, they'll hurt my children."

"Before they know what's happening, it'll be over. Our man doesn't take prisoners."

"I believe that. Not because you're telling me. I've already seen what he can do. But the odds at San Bartolomeo won't be six to one. They'll be thirty or forty to one. If he doesn't manage it, if my children aren't returned to me, I'll give you nothing. Do you understand? Nothing. No tapes. No testimony. I don't care what you do to me. You can put me in jail forever. Or take me out and shoot me. Or turn me loose and let the Murillos do it for you. Without my boys there is nothing."

Brognola set the tray of food on the conference table in front of her. "Better eat something," he said. "You've got to stay strong."

Needless to say, neither of them had slept.

She picked up a glass of lemonade and took a sip through the straw.

Brognola didn't know if she had been acting before, but he had the sense that she definitely wasn't acting now. In different ways, they both were trapped in the mesh of the operation's gears. Events would grind inevitably to some conclusion, good or bad. That conclusion was beyond their control.

"I love my children," she told him suddenly. "I love them more than my own life."

"I understand."

What he wanted to ask was, "Then how on earth did you let yourself get involved in all this?" But the words didn't cross his lips. The puzzle of Yovana Ortiz remained a puzzle. He didn't want to push his luck and upset her again. Whatever her reasons, they had to be overwhelming. And private.

Brognola glanced at the ruined electronic equipment. She had really trashed it—without apology. Ortiz was used to doing exactly as she liked, when she liked. Up until now, when it really mattered.

She put the glass on the table and stared into it for a long moment. "I want you to know something else," she said. "I understand that your people are putting their lives on the line for me and my children. Strangers are risking everything to help me. I don't want you to think that I'm ungrateful for their effort, or for yours. It's just that I'm so scared something bad is going to happen to them. I'm more scared than I have ever been in all my life. Can you understand that?"

Brognola was surprised. Taken aback even. The last things he expected from her were gratitude and humility. He concealed his reaction, however. "I understand perfectly," he said.

He didn't give her more false assurances. He couldn't bring himself to do that. His stomach churned. He took a couple of antacids from the tube in his pocket, popped them in his mouth and crunched them softly into powder.

11

The difficulty of the terrain made Mack Bolan's pace erratic, at best. He ran down the hills, but the steep upgrades slowed him to a trudging crawl. Though he pushed himself hard, he drove his body at a level he could sustain for hours, like a marathoner jogging through seven levels of Hell. Because of the effort he was expending under the sun's broiling heat, his body's moisture loss was tremendous. He tried to ration his drinking water to make it last. He should've carried more. A lot more. But the additional weight might have been the straw that broke the camel's back.

Two hours into his trek, he finished and discarded the lone bottle he'd brought.

When his thirst started raging again, he picked up a flat, smooth pebble, brushed it off and put it in his mouth. Sucking on it made him salivate, which temporarily eased the problem.

Not once had the morning's ordeal made him question what he was doing, not once had he asked himself why. He knew why. He had signed on for this mission because he believed in its ultimate goal. He hadn't been ordered by the President to take it. When it came to missions, Mack Bolan had the right of refusal, always. However, the opportunity to bring down a major drug lord was not something he could easily turn down. The Executioner had a long history of taking on precisely that kind of criminal scumbag. Taking them on and wiping them out. The rescue of the Ortiz woman's children from an animal like Ramon Murillo was the icing on the cake.

Bolan knelt in the scant shade of a tall saguaro cactus. He unclipped the battery-powered, microminiaturized Global Positioning System unit from his harness and checked his progress. According to satellite tracking data, his current latitude and longitude put the rancho somewhere over the next mountain. The pebble clicked against the back of his teeth as he took stock of his own physical condition. His legs still felt strong. His head was clear. The effects of dehydration were, so far, not evident.

The Baja sun was directly overhead as the Executioner slowly climbed the backside of the last, towering hill. The going was so steep that he had to take it in a series of tight switchbacks, zigzags that traversed the crumbling gullies. As he neared the crest, he unslung his sniper rifle. Upon reaching the summit he immediately dropped to his knees, then belly-crawled to the rim and looked over the edge.

Spread out below him was a landscape of beige dirt and rock. From his vantage point he could see the rear of the Murillos's rancho, its stuccoed perimeter wall and, farther out, the silver line of the steel fence and the arch of the main gate. In the distance he could hear gasoline-powered engines revving. They sounded like motorcycles or chainsaws.

He took a pair of Zeiss minibinoculars from his pants pocket. Mindful of the sun's angle and the possibility of a telltale lens flash, he surveyed the killzone. The sprawling, two-story hacienda was the size of a hotel. It was done up in Old Mexico style—rows of sawed-off, wooden ceiling beams protruded through the brown exterior wall, marking the top of each story. A palm-leaf thatched porch protected the ground-floor rear of the building. The upper-story rooms had a row of recessed balconies likewise shaded their full length with awnings made of mats of palm.

On the roof of the building, in one corner opposite a huge white satellite dish, was a little, open-sided, palm-roofed hut. Bolan concentrated on it, adjusting the focus ring of his minibinocs to pull in the maximum detail. After a moment, he was able to pick out the silhouettes of two men inside the structure in the shadows.

Riflemen.

Trying to stay cool.

From their position, they had a 360-degree free-fire zone.

About 150 yards to the right of the rancho was a paved airstrip long enough to land a small jet. No jet was in evidence. A single-engine Cessna stood parked beside the runway. Next to a small hangar was another open-sided, roofed area; in the shade were ten rows of bright blue, fifty-five-gallon aviation fuel drums. Closer to the rancho, abutting the far side of the stuccoed wall was a garage outbuilding. He could see the line of vehicles parked under the carport's roof.

There were no guards or workers walking outside. It was too damned hot.

As he scanned the area downrange, the high-pitched sound of an engine grew louder. Bolan swung the binoculars toward the source of the sound. A three-wheeled, all-terrain vehicle popped out of a distant arroyo, raising a dust cloud as it bounded over the plain in the direction of the rancho. It was one of three. Though he couldn't see the others, he could make out their spiraling dusty plumes. The Executioner lowered the binoculars, noting the lighter brown lines that crosshatched the landscape. It was obvious that the Murillos used ATVs as their patrol vehicles. He raised the field glasses again.

The driver of the lead ATV wore a big, broad-brimmed straw hat to shield his head and shoulders from the sun. He also wore gloves and wraparound sunglasses. Slung over his right shoulder was an M-16. A walkie-talkie was clipped to his handlebars and a small ice chest tied on a rack behind his seat.

At almost the same instant, the other two ATVs appeared over a low ridgeline. About a hundred feet apart, they turned away from each other in wide arcs, heading for the rancho from opposing directions.

Bolan lay there and watched the mobile sentries complete two patrol circuits to make sure that their routes were regular and not random. The paths they took varied, but only slightly, due to the irregular terrain. The vehicles weren't going all that fast, maybe twenty miles an hour. Going fast over such broken ground would be painful, a bone- and kidney-jarring experience, especially over the course of a four-hour watch. The ATV drivers were traveling just fast enough to keep themselves cool.

It was a boring, hot, dusty job.

A job where the mind tended to wander because there was nothing new to see.

On his next pass, the guy in the big hat pulled in beside the aircraft hangar and stopped under the palm canopy. Comfortably in the shade, the driver unslung his assault rifle, unzipped his pants and started to relieve himself.

The angle—a thirty-degree downhill shot—was excellent. The line of fire was clear.

Bolan shouldered the M-89 sniper rifle. Looking over the top of the telescope, he watched one of the other ATVs rumble through the opening in the rancho's left wall and start its tour of the inner perimeter. The wall and the rancho blocked that driver's view of the hangar area. Over the whine of his own engine, the sentry would have a hard time hearing the gunshot. The third sentry had already completed his circuit and was headed in the opposite direction.

The Executioner spit out the pebble he'd been nursing, fitted the bolt-action rifle's stock to his shoulder, flipped up the lens cap on the telescopic sight, and dropped the safety.

There was no wind whatsoever.

The air was nice and dry.

He used the Leupold's bullet drop compensator to adjust for the distance to target. The cartridge nestled against the firing pin was a full-power load, 2,600 feet per second, 2,500-foot pounds of muzzle energy. Subsonic loads weren't necessary, thanks to the Arconus suppressor. Its radical new design dispersed instead of muffling the sound barrier-breaking gun-crack, making it impossible for targets downrange to locate its source. Had Bolan gone with subsonic ammunition, the bullet's knockdown power would have degraded to a mere 390-foot pounds, with accompanying loss of accuracy—at his current distance of four hundred yards, it would have been like throwing rocks. Bolan snugged the rifle's stock deeper into his shoulder and lined up the shot, dropping the top of the sight post a tad to account for the downward angle.

The driver had finished relieving himself against the side of a barrel and was in the act of rezipping his fly when the Executioner edged the trigger past the break point. The firing pin snapped crisply and the heavy rifle boomed, bucking hard against his shoulder. He rode the recoil, automatically cycling the smooth-as-butter bolt, jacking a follow-up round into the chamber.

In the scope's view field, Bolan watched the driver as he spun sideways, slamming into one of the canopy's support posts and going down hard. From the way his arms flew away from the chest, stretching wide as if in an embrace, Bolan knew he'd scored a central torso hit. The man dropped out of sight, but the soles of his desert boots stuck out from the row of fuel barrels. There was no frantic kicking of legs, no digging in of the toes, not even a faint, spastic tremor of the feet. The boots lay still.

Bolan swung his sights onto the hacienda's rooftop.

Hearing the gunshot, one of the riflemen stationed there had quickly moved to the edge of the roof. He was looking the wrong way. Silhouetted in the blinding glare of the sun, the drug soldier lifted a massive pair of binoculars to his eyes. He didn't seem particularly excited by the fireworks. It wasn't unusual for high-powered gunshots to sound from that direction—big-game hunters, mostly rich gringos, sometimes worked the desolate range for trophy mountain sheep.

The Executioner waited until the second man came out of the shade, his long gun in hand and stepped up beside his partner. When they were side by side, Bolan tightened on the trigger. The sniper rifle bucked. Half a second later the guy with the binoculars toppled, falling below the lip of the roof.

The second rifleman just stood there, gun in hand, frozen in shock and disbelief. Before he could think about moving, Bolan sent another 168-grain slug screaming his way. Then it was too late to think. A puff of pink haloed his head, glistening in the sunlight. It hung there for a second or two, even as his corpse dropped out of sight.

The Executioner recapped the scope at once.

Inside the rancho compound, the second ATV was continuing its circuit of the perimeter. Despite three gunshots in fairly rapid succession, it didn't stop or slow.

Bolan picked up his binoculars again and scanned the second-story balcony. With the sun's hard glare, the palm awning and the recessed porches, the shadows were virtually impenetrable. If there were more stationary sentries on duty there, he couldn't pick them out. He got the impression from the way the ATV drivers were working, or not working, that the place wasn't on high alert. There was the possibility, of course, that the Murillos had pulled all their forces back inside the villa to make a stand. It seemed much more likely to him that they weren't expecting an attack of any consequence. Maybe because they were counting on one of their bribed government officials to give them a warning well in advance? After all, that's what they were paid for.

It appeared that the Murillos weren't overly concerned about the tall stranger who'd landed on their beach.

The Executioner had already neutralized six of their men.

And the hurting hadn't even started yet.

Bolan shoulder-slung the rifle and darted over the crest of the mountain. He crossed twenty yards of broken ground, then jumped into a gully that led downslope, but angled away from the rancho to the west. The ditch was only about five feet deep, so he ran in a half crouch, keeping his head as low as possible. The gully widened as it neared the base of the hill, turning into an arroyo. The Executioner followed the sandy wash until he was on the far side of the rancho's airstrip.

Then he stopped and listened. The sounds of the ATVs were jumbled; he couldn't tell which way they were headed. There wasn't time to wait and see. He'd left two dead men on the rancho's roof. He had to penetrate the building before they were discovered.

He scrambled out of the arroyo and crossed the broad stretch of unprotected ground on a dead run, keeping the hangar between himself and the rancho. When he reached the back of the hangar, he dashed to the corner nearest the fuel dump. Peering around it, he could see the parked ATV and the big-hatted driver lying on his face in the shade. Spanish voices erupted from the walkie-talkie strapped to the ATV's handlebars.

In the same instant, Bolan realized that the engines on the other side of the hangar had grown abruptly louder. The tall double door was open a crack. He slipped inside. It wasn't just a hangar. It was a shipment point for Samosa's drugs. A warehouse loaded with bales of prepackaged marijuana and bundled blocks of cocaine and heroin.

The ATV pulled up outside the hangar, brakes squealing as it came to a stop. Bolan couldn't give the driver time to find his friend and sound an alarm. As soon as the vehicle stopped, he jumped out of the doorway, his sound-suppressed Beretta in his hand.

The sentry, who wore a cap with a handkerchief tucked under the headband, foreign legion style, to protect his neck and ears, was just climbing off his ATV. Bolan caught him in mid-dismount, standing on one foot. He was still connected to the engine's kill switch by a thong on his wrist. His M-16 was hanging from his shoulder. Useless.

The Executioner shot him in the chest, throat and face as he advanced, walking the 9 mm hollowpoints up the target. He kept coming even as the sentry crumpled. As Bolan rounded the front of the vehicle the man slipped to the ground.

Bolan continued on, heading for the fuel barrels. As he walked, he took a small ballistic nylon pouch from his combat harness and undid the cover, exposing a gray wad of C-4 high explosive, wires, blasting cap and a remote detonator switch. He wedged the package between a pair of the barrels. Then he unsheathed his SEAL knife and knelt. With a single, powerful thrust, he punctured one of the full drums near its base. When he pulled the blade free of the steel, a stream of airplane gas jetted into the sand. In a few minutes the whole area would be saturated.

After wiping the blade on his pants, he resheathed it. Then he charged into the open, heading for the warning markers painted on the tarmac at the end of the landing field. He crossed the airstrip, dashing past a pair of tattered, orange wind socks that hung limply from their poles. His choice of route wasn't as wild as it seemed. The side of the hacienda that faced him had no balconies and very few windows. And the shooters on the roof were in no condition to report a suspicious armed prowler.

He ducked under the garage's carport. For the moment at least, he was completely out of sight of the rancho. He unslung the M-89 sniper rifle and leaned it against the wall.

He wouldn't be carrying it any farther. The Beretta and the MAC-10 were his close-quarters weapons of choice.

Bolan took a moment to look over the collection of vehicles. There were three hammered full-size pickups, and a dual-rear wheel stake truck, obviously all used for ranch work. Parked beside them was a desert camouflage Humvee. Its hood was tipped up, which wasn't a good sign.

He walked over to the pair of new four-wheel-drive Chevy Suburbans. He opened the door of the dark green one and found the keys in the ignition. He turned the key partway and a chime tone sounded. The fuel gauge needle rose to three-quarters full.

It would do just fine.

Bolan put the keys in his pocket and shut the door.

Dropping to his back, he squirmed beneath the undercarriage of the other Suburban. He nicked the brake lines with his SEAL knife, then squirmed out again.

Gathering his gear, Bolan sprinted away from the garage, heading south along the outside of the perimeter wall. There he stopped and peered around the edge.

The third sentry was swinging toward the rancho, apparently oblivious to the fates of his compadres.

The Executioner waited until the man was out of sight, then ran along the front of the compound to the wall opening that faced the rancho's entrance. Bolan was counting on the gunner sticking to his routine. He was also counting on him not to try to make contact with his fellow sentries.

The howl of the ATV's engine suddenly reverberated off the sides of the rancho. The driver was inside the compound, making his tour. Bolan crouched at the base of the wall. The sound of the ATV grew louder as the third sentry accelerated toward the break in the front wall.

In order to make the turn after he slipped through the opening, the driver had to drop his speed.

When he downshifted, Bolan stood and raised his weapon.

When the ATV roared around the corner, the driver came face-to-face with the muzzle of the Beretta 93-R. He reacted instantly and instinctively, cutting the front wheel hard over, trying to swerve out of the way.

Bolan had anticipated the move. He stood his ground and, leading his target, fired three times in rapid succession. The flurry of gunshots were inaudible over the motor's howl. The driver's head snapped to one side, his fingers slipped from the handles' grips and he fell backward off the seat, crashing to the dirt. The off-road vehicle's motor sputtered and died as the ignition cut out. The ATV rolled to a stop.

A dead man's switch for real.

The ensuing silence was deafening.

Someone was bound to notice the missing whine of engines and come out to investigate. Unclipping the MAC-10 from the lanyard around his neck, the Executioner sucked in a deep breath.

It was time to live large.

12

Ramon Murillo sat on a folding chair at the ramshackle cantina's little metal table, jingling a handful of long carpenter's nails. Blueprints of the ex-president of Mexico's mansion were spread out in front of him, as were street maps of the area.

"You realize we'll only have one chance to get the bitch," Murillo said to the man with the pencil mustache sitting across the table from him. "If we fail, she'll be spirited across the border, and then it will be too late. What I'm saying is, there's more than a whole lot of money at stake here."

The other man knew exactly what he meant. The half-smoked cigarette trembled in his fingers as he raised it to his lips.

Ramon Murillo had worked hard to cultivate his reputation as a murderously sick son of a bitch. He had consciously searched for a style that would set him apart from all the other drug thugs in Baja. He didn't want just a clever nickname; they were a dime a dozen. His brother Roberto's nom de guerre was symbolic, "The Whip" meaning the instrument of power and domination. "Three Nails" was something more, an actuality. A calling card. It proved without a doubt that he was crazier and more bloodthirsty than anyone else. The mere sound of his name made his enemies shudder and piss themselves.

Crucifixion had a special resonance in Mexico because

of the stronghold of the Catholic church. Over and above the infliction of terrible pain and disfigurement, the act itself because of its history was an abomination, an insult to God Himself. And in Mexico a man who dared to spit in the face of God was a man to be feared by all.

Murillo had no particular ritual that he followed. He didn't employ special nails for the procedure. He used commonplace, hardware-store nails. He never sharpened them, either. For a hammer he used whatever was available—a chunk of rock, a broken chair leg, the heel of his shoe. One time he'd used the base of a metal lamp.

He'd never nailed anybody to a real cross. He just tacked them up anyplace he found handy. Garage doors. Gateposts. Any suitable expanse of interior wall. Because it could sometimes take days for a crucified person to die, he always shot them in the head. Three Nails never left any witnesses to his crimes.

"What have you learned about the men who have her?" he asked the man across the table.

"Our DEA informant hasn't turned up anything. He says they aren't FBI or DEA. We've taken some telephoto pictures of a couple of them going in and out the front doors."

He took copies of black-and-white photos from an envelope and passed them across to his patron.

They showed lean, athletic-looking, middle-aged men with short haircuts. "CIA, then?" Murillo speculated.

"Our informant doesn't think so." The man tapped the top photo. "This is a top-notch security team."

"How top-notch? Secret Service?"

"That's exactly what I think. And if that's who they are, we're going to have trouble taking out the woman even after they leave the mansion."

"Talk me through the layout."

"We have the above-ground area completely contained," the man said. "We can block off all the exit streets with vehicles. But if we tackle them on top of the mesa, it means a firefight. A public spectacle. Innocent dead."

Murillo wasn't bothered by that. "You're saying that we might not win a firefight?"

"If they are Secret Service, and their vehicles are armored, bullet- and bombproof, they could hold us off long enough for help to arrive."

"What about the tunnel exit?"

"We stand a much better chance there. No one is supposed to know it even exists. It opens onto the slope at the base of the mesa. It's camouflaged with rock and brush and looks like the end of a sewer or culvert pipe. Twenty feet inside the pipe is a steel door. Anyone leaving by that route has to walk more than thirty yards across unprotected ground to reach a vehicle. There's a lot of foot traffic in the area. The path connects to the back of an open public market."

"We have to make them use the tunnel exit, then," Murillo said. "Can you arrange for that to happen?"

"Of course. We can frontal assault the mansion. It'll cost more money. There will be death benefits. Some of our people are going to go down. And it will take me more time to arrange for the extra manpower."

"You have half an hour."

The man knew better than to protest.

Murillo played with his spikes for a moment, rolling them in his hand. "I know exactly how I want the assassination carried out," he said.

The man looked at the nails.

Murillo smiled and shook his head. "No, no, not for this one. Get me two pounds of plastic explosive and a detonator."

"Do you want a wireless remote? Do you want infrared? What's the range going to be?"

"I won't be needing a remote. I want the C-4 connected

PLAY
RUN
FOR THE
ROSES

and get
THREE FREE GIFTS!
HOW TO PLAY:

1. With a coin, carefully scratch off the silver box at the right. Then check the claim chart t see what we have for you — **2 FREE BOOKS** and a **FREE GIFT**—**ALL YOURS FREE**

2. Send back the card and you'll receive two hot-off-the-press Gold Eagle® novels. These books have a cover price of $4.50 or more each in the U.S. and $5.25 or more each in Canada, but they are yours to keep absolutely free.

3. There's no catch. You're under no obligation to buy anything. We charge nothing — ZERO — for your first shipment. And you don't have to make any minimum number of purchases — not even one!

4. The fact is, thousands of readers enjoy receiving books by mail from the Gold Eagle Reader Service™. They like the convenience of home delivery...they like getting the best new novels months before they're available in stores... and they love our discount prices!

5. We hope that after receiving your free books you'll want to remain a subscriber. But the choice is yours — to continue or cancel, any time at all! So why not take us up on our invitation, with no risk of any kind. You'll be glad you did!

This surprise mystery gift
Could be yours **FREE** —
When you play
RUN for the ROSES

The Gold Eagle Reader Service™ — Here's how it works:

Accepting your 2 free books and gift places you under no obligation to buy anything. You may keep the books and gift and return the shipping statement marked "cancel." If you do not cancel, about a month later we'll send you 6 additional novels and bill you just $26.70* — that's a saving of 15% off the cover price of all 6 books! And there's no extra charge for shipping! You may cancel at any time, but if you choose to continue, every other month we'll send you 6 more books, which you may either purchase at the discount price or return to us and cancel your subscription.

*Terms and prices subject to change without notice. Sales tax applicable in N.Y. Canadian residents will be charged applicable provincial taxes and GST.

If offer card is missing write to: Gold Eagle Reader Service, 3010 Walden Ave., P.O. Box 1867, Buffalo NY 14240-1867

BUSINESS REPLY MAIL
FIRST-CLASS MAIL   PERMIT NO. 717   BUFFALO, NY

POSTAGE WILL BE PAID BY ADDRESSEE

GOLD EAGLE READER SERVICE
3010 WALDEN AVE
PO BOX 1867
BUFFALO NY 14240-9952

NO POSTAGE
NECESSARY
IF MAILED
IN THE
UNITED STATES

to a single-button detonator with no more than a foot or so of wire.''

''I don't understand.''

''You don't have to. Just do as I say.'' Ramon scraped back his chair and rose to his feet. ''And do it quickly.''

13

Bolan sprinted back around the outside of the perimeter wall, to the break on the west side. He paused there just long enough to make sure no one had stepped out of the rancho into the inner courtyard. He dashed to the side of the building, then turned left, toward the rear entrance. Stopping at the corner, he reclipped the MAC-10 to the lanyard around his neck. He took a mini-grappling hook from a pouch on his harness and uncoiled its thin nylon rope at his feet. Bolan swung the hook around his head, working up some speed, then launched it almost straight up. The weighted claw head arced over the roof near the back corner of the rancho, landing with a soft thud. He tightened up on the line, dragging the grappling hook over the inside of the roof's raised lip until its sharp spines caught and sank in.

The Executioner tested the hook's set twice, pulling with all his weight. Satisfied that it would hold him, he started to climb the rope hand over hand. When he came level with the second-floor balcony, he used his booted soles to edge his way around the corner. Pushing off hard, he stepped onto the rail and released the cord. He ducked under the palm awning, and as he dropped softly to the balcony floor, the stubby Ingram was already back in his hands.

Ten feet from the rail, under the overhang of the awning and the building's roof, the rear balcony had four tall archways evenly spaced along its length. They had no doors. Bolan moved to the nearest entrance. It took a few seconds for his eyes to adjust to the deep shade. While he waited, he listened hard. He could hear a television or radio. The sound was muffled, but very close. When his eyes adjusted, he could see that the balcony opened onto a long corridor with a tiled floor. The hallway offered access to four doors along this side of the rancho.

The Executioner crossed the corridor and put his back to the facing wall. The noise was coming from the corner room. It sounded like a baseball game. There were other voices, too, all male. Arguing in Spanish.

He had no idea how many drug soldiers were on the other side of the arched door. And he didn't care. Five or twenty-five, it didn't matter. However many of the opposition there were, he was going through the doorway and over them.

A sudden wave of cheers exploded from the TV. The announcer said, "That one's going, going, gone! That puppy's a four-bagger, folks, it's out of here!"

There were loud whistles and groans from the men on the other side of the door.

The door's handle wasn't a knob, but a thumb latch with a curved, wrought-iron grip. Bolan took it in his left hand and, in a single, smoothly flowing motion, lifted the latch, shoved the door inward and jumped over the threshold. He came to rest on the balls of his feet, knees slightly bent, with the sound-suppressed submachine gun braced in both hands.

The cheering on the big-screen TV continued, the cheering in the room cut off as if by a switch.

The Executioner soaked up the scene in half a heartbeat.

There were four Mexican men seated along the wall to his left, all of them shocked into drop-jawed silence. One sat on a recliner, the other three on a long couch. The guys on the couch had their heels propped up on a low table.

They ate from individual ceramic bowls of fried tortilla chips clutched to their chests. The frozen faces of the off-duty guards were lighted by the big-screen TV on the opposite wall.

Recovering from their surprise at the sudden entrance of a war-painted man with an SMG, the Murillo soldiers simultaneously made a mad scramble for their own guns.

The Executioner responded by flattening the MAC-10's trigger, sweeping a line of fire at waist height across half the room. Black Talon rounds clawed through the man in the armchair. The impacts slammed him into the seat and held him there. On the couch, the next guy half rose from his seat only to be met by a flurry of slugs across his chest, stitching him from armpit to armpit. His face convulsed in a grimace of agony; the snack bowl in his hands shattered, sending tortilla chips flying.

The two men at the other end of the couch managed to lean forward and get their hands on their guns, but before they could raise and aim them, 9 mm slugs from the Ingram whipped across their faces. Their heads came apart, violently. The backs of their skulls exploded, splattering brains across the off-white wall behind them and the blade of the fan overhead, which then sprayed all four walls and the ceiling with droplets of pink.

It was over in seconds.

Bolan had expended thirty rounds, a full clip. The floor was littered with spent shell casings, the room fogged with gunsmoke and aerosolized gore. Bolan dumped the empty mag onto the floor and cracked in a fresh one. He chambered the first round in the stack, then crossed the room with his finger resting lightly on the trigger. He checked the bathroom to make sure it was unoccupied.

Sitting on a stand beside the TV was a covered carafe of water. The sight of it reminded him how thirsty he was. He needed to rehydrate. He set the MAC-10 down on the stand and removed the carafe's lid. He drank straight from the jug, trying hard not to gulp down too much air. The water wasn't cold, but it tasted good. He drank deep and long.

Bolan was still drinking when a short guy in a gray T-shirt and a black ballistic nylon shoulder holster waltzed through the door. As he entered the room, he asked in Spanish, "Who's ahead?"

The question ended in a strangled croak.

The short man's eyes widened as he took in the total carnage around him. The drug soldier took an automatic, half step backward. He opened his mouth to yell a warning, and as he did, he reached for the butt of the high capacity autopistol suspended under his left armpit.

The Executioner opened his right hand and let the water jug fall. He didn't lunge for the Ingram. Instinctively, he knew it was too far away.

His Beretta cleared leather at the same instant as the soldier freed his Smith & Wesson. After that, it was no contest.

The 9 mm round jolted the gunner backward, headfirst. The slug passed through the back of the man's skull and sailed out the open doorway before whacking into something solid. And the short guy dropped as if all his strings had been cut, toppling with arms outstretched across the threshold.

Bolan leaned down and grabbed the man by his still-kicking feet and dragged him into the room. Then he stepped out through the doorway. The sun was blinding. The center of the building had no roof. The rooms on the second story opened onto an interior balcony that ran around the entire floor and overlooked the atrium below. Across the gap, he could see the balcony on the other side of the courtyard.

The Executioner stepped quickly to the rail before him. The blue swimming pool below was cut in two, divided by sunlight and shadow. At the other end of the patio, he saw the children. They were sitting on the white flagstones with their heads close together, playing a game. The salsa music came from behind them. A boom box stood on a low table beside a chaise lounge. The lawn chair was partially in deep shade, but Bolan recognized the man sitting on it from DEA photos. It was *El Azote*. Roberto Murillo. Seated around him at the other patio tables and on the edge of the fountain's rim, were twelve heavily armed guards.

Movement on the balcony opposite caught Bolan's eye. He looked up at a fat guy with a slicked-back, black ponytail. Perhaps alerted by the slap of the single bullet hitting a cornerstone, perhaps caught in the middle of a routine patrol of the building, the drug thug saw him, too, and reacted at once. He started to draw a SIG from the holster on his hip. The large-frame semiauto pistol looked like a toy in his hand.

Before the man could clear leather and get the shot lined up, Bolan braced against the balcony's concrete support post and, dropping fire selector to single shot, took aim with a two-handed grip. With a precise, light touch on the trigger, he fired once. The Black Talon round flat-lined across the open space and caught the sentry very high in the chest, just under his throat.

At the stunning impact, the overweight man staggered back, his gun hand still coming up. Somewhere in the arc between waist and shoulder, his fingers lost their grip on the SIG's rubber-clad butt, and the heavy autopistol flew out of his hand. It cleared the balcony rail by more than a yard and then sailed deep into the open space over the courtyard. The pistol spun slowly end over end as it fell.

The soldier leaned forward, watching helplessly as the weapon plummeted. It landed with a loud splash in the shallow end of the swimming pool.

So much for stealth.

The Executioner stepped forward, thumbed the MAC-

10's fire selector switch to full auto and nosed the muzzle over the rail.

THE SOUND OF little Pedro's shrill laughter resounding in the courtyard made Roberto Murillo stiffen. To him it was like fingernails scraping on a blackboard or the whine of a dentist's drill. Even on his best of days, Murillo wasn't a kid person. Temporarily baby-sitting children, even the children of his all-powerful Patron, wasn't his cup of tea. He cranked up the volume on the boom box beside his chaise lounge, glaring daggers at the boys.

Unlike Ramon, Roberto had never been able to conceal his overwhelming distaste for Ortiz's children, and for the mollycoddling they required. He was certain that the boys could sense his dislike for them, and that they returned it in spades. That the spoiled little bastards would be gone from his sight forever by nightfall was one of two things that kept him from having them both strangled on the spot. The other thing that stayed his hand, of course, was how much Samosa would frown on the unauthorized murders of his only sons and heirs.

Part of the pressure Murillo was feeling at that moment had to do with the still-missing Radon and his obsession for complete control of his own environment. The self-appointed *generalisimo,* Murillo didn't like unexplained phenomena of any kind, and particularly when so much hung in the balance.

The last word from the Panga he had sent out after the Radon had come in thirty minutes earlier. They had radioed back that they were almost to the entrance of Bahia Concepción, just south of Mulegé. They said they had found no sign of either boat.

The disappearance of his people and their boat made no sense to Murillo. Unless Paolo and the others had been lured by the stranger into an ambush up the coast. This possibility raised more questions than it answered.

While the Mexican authorities on his payroll would never participate in a preemptive strike on his Loreto compound, he could visualize the U.S. government, through one of its law enforcement agencies, staging just such a raid. He was confident that no attack was coming because his informants on both sides of the border would have certainly warned him that a large-scale operation against him was under way. But, even assuming that something had gone wrong, there was no warning that the rancho had been targeted, what would taking out the Radon accomplish?

The reduction of his security force by three?

The destruction of a single boat?

In terms of strategic value, the men and the Radon were inconsequential. And the failure of the boat to return to the cove could give away the impending attack. It would at least put the rancho on high alert. In Murillo's experience, the Feds weren't that stupid. And they were extremely cautious when it came to operations off their own soil.

The disappearance of the man the Radon had been sent out to catch and eliminate also concerned him. What had happened to the stranger and his boat? Had he turned east and tried to run across the Sea of Cortez to the Mexican mainland to escape Paolo and the others? That would explain part of the current situation. If the Radon had turned east and its radio had gone out, Paolo wouldn't have been able to report back. Trouble was, there was no way the Panga the stranger was driving could escape the much-faster boat. It should have caught up with him in a matter of a mile or two.

No matter how Murillo turned the available facts, he could make no sense of them.

Again, Pedro shrieked with laughter. Murillo winced at the shrill sound. The look on his face was by turns irritated, bitter, jealous, seething and anything but kind. Ortiz's precious boys were an abomination to him. They had everything: a pretty mother who loved them, a rich, powerful father who wanted them near him. Thinking about that made Murillo feel a crushing sense of depression. He was about to tell the guards to take the boys inside out of the sun, away from him, when something fell into the pool.

Out of the corner of his eye, he saw the thing drop from a height of maybe fifteen feet. It looked dark and a little bigger than the size of a man's open hand. And it made a heavy splash when it hit the water.

"What the hell was that?" he demanded, sitting bolt upright. His first thought was that a gull or a pelican, or even a sea eagle flying over the rancho, had dropped something from its beak that had ended up in the pool. It had happened before with gulls carrying clams. "Get it out of the pool!"

The closest drug soldier walked to the edge of the pool and looked down. "It's a gun," he said in amazement. "Somebody dropped a gun." He bent his head back and looked up at the second-story balcony. As he did, something sizzled past his right ear and zipped into the water. He cranked his head just in time to see an automatic weapon winking at him from above the second-floor rail. A string of slugs streaked into and through him, spilling him backward into the pool.

Splay-armed, the man made a sizable splash, sank a couple of feet, then bobbed back to the surface, oozing clouds of blood from the holes in his chest and arms. Like his mouth, his eyes were wide open.

Murillo launched himself up from the chaise lounge. His first thought was for the boys. Not because he cared about them, personally, but because they were valuable objects. He grabbed Juanito and Pedro by their arms and roughly jerked them back from the rectangle of sunlight and under the cover of a patio table and umbrella.

How did someone get through the rancho's defenses? he asked himself. How did they penetrate the layers of defense that he had designed? The cove, the steel fence, the ATVs and the perimeter wall were all constructed to hold back an attacking force long enough to alert the rancho. The soft layers of defense were meant to collapse, one after the other, giving the rancho time to ready itself for siege.

This can't be happening, he thought. But the dead man floating in the pool was proof positive that it was.

At his scattering soldiers, who were also moving to cover away from the middle of the courtyard, he cried, "Upstairs! You! You! You! Get up there and get them!"

Three of his men rushed for the enclosed staircase that led to the second floor. Reaching it, they paused on either side of the entry. One of the drug soldiers stuck his head around the corner, looking up the stairs for intruders. He jerked back at once and nodded to the others. It was all clear. All three men charged up the steps with guns drawn.

Roberto Murillo didn't see the stun grenades rolling down the stairs toward his guards. He didn't hear them as they bounded over the stone steps. But he couldn't miss the cries of horror his men let loose a split second before the earthshaking detonations.

Blinding white light erupted out of the stairwell. The explosion was so violent in the confined space that it shook the rancho's walls and made plaster dust rain from the ceilings. It literally blew the three soldiers out of the staircase opening. They landed, sprawling on their backs and frantically tried to regain their feet.

A torrent of suppressed autofire raged out of the stairwell, stitching over the fallen men, chewing them up where they lay.

A pistol, flung away by one of the downed soldiers, skittered across the patio. It bounced into the legs of the table Murillo was hiding behind and stopped. He picked up the Smith & Wesson semiauto.

"How many? How many?" he shouted at his men.

No one answered. Because no one knew.

"Close on them! Go on!" Murillo bellowed.

Five of the guards dashed to the stairwell entrance and started taking turns blindly firing up at the second-floor landing.

They only fired for a second or two before turning tail. They dived under tables, ducked behind lawn chairs.

Two cylindrical-shaped grenades rolled down the steps onto the patio. Murillo averted his eyes just in time to avoid the brilliant flash. With an ear-splitting, near-simultaneous thunderclap, all three grenades detonated. The shock wave blew over tables and exploded the plate glass windows on the ground floor.

It took a full minute for Murillo's ears to stop ringing. Then he heard strings of gunshots and shouts from the second floor. The explosions had finally roused the off-duty soldiers upstairs from their siestas. Now they would make a fight of it.

An instant later, a tremendous boom erupted over their heads. Metal fragments whined through the air, clattering into the deck, tables and walls. Murillo ducked, and as he did, a section of the second-floor balcony broke free of its stanchions and dropped with a tremendous crash into the shallow end of the pool. A cloud of dust and smoke rushed down from above, sweeping over his position.

"You four," Murillo said, half choking on the dust as he waved at the men nearest to him, "you come with me. We've got to get Don Jorge's boys out of here."

As the fusillade resumed over their heads, they retreated around the atrium wall to the entrance to the rancho's spacious front room. Doors at both ends of the long room opened onto stairwells leading to the upper floor. Murillo sent a man to guard each flight of steps. Then he pushed the boys into the fireplace's massive hearth, pushed them over the log grate to the back of the firebox, where they'd be safe from stray bullets.

After seemingly interminable minutes of clattering thunder, the gunfire upstairs abruptly ceased.

Seconds passed.

Then Murillo cupped hand to mouth and shouted to the five men hiding behind the patio's fountain. "Go up!" he ordered them. "Go up and make sure it's over!" He waved at them impatiently.

One after another, they disappeared up the stairwell.

Murillo glanced over at the children huddled in the fireplace. Juanito had a protective arm around his younger brother's shoulders. Both of them were crying.

His gaze shifted to the rancho's main entrance. The heavy, iron-bound, wooden doors stood slightly ajar. He didn't want to have to retreat through them. In order to reach the perimeter wall and cover, he would have to cross a wide stretch of open ground. If the enemy wasn't defeated, if they had control of the front balconies, that route would be suicide.

The silence from upstairs continued.

With every passing second, Murillo's optimism grew.

"Do you see anything?" he asked the men he'd stationed at the ends of the room. They peeked up their respective staircases and quickly ducked back.

"Nothing," said one.

"No one," said the other.

Then gunfire broke out once more above them. Horrendous streams of bullets. Then an explosion rocked the rancho to its foundations. Followed by bloodcurdling screams of agony.

It wasn't over, yet.

Not by a long shot.

14

The sound-suppressed MAC-10 stuttered, chugging against Mack Bolan's two-handed grip. A bright arc of brass spewed from its clacking bolt as he rained lead on the man who had discovered the gun that had fallen into the shallow end of the swimming pool. The tight circle of fire sent him crashing over backward into the water.

From around the courtyard, excited yells broke out as the gunmen realized they were under attack. Confusion wasn't only the Executioner's chief ally—it was his only ally. He sprinted for the enclosed staircase forty feet ahead, which led from the balcony to the ground. He arrived just in time to hear the tramp of heavy feet running up the stairwell toward him. Bolan jerked a pair of Thunderflash stun grenades from the straps of his combat harness. After yanking the safety pins and letting the grip safeties fly off, he lobbed the grenades down the staircase.

Below him, someone let out a hoarse cry. The Executioner imagined the look on the face of the first man up the stairs. The look when he saw the objects bouncing down at him, when he recognized what they were. Would he do an abrupt about-face, colliding with the men coming up behind him? Or would he freeze, eyes shut tight and let the stun bombs roll past?

Run or freeze, freeze or run, it made no difference. A second later the Thunderflashes detonated. In the confined space of the stairwell, the near-simultaneous concussions acted like a cannon charge, blowing the guards off their feet and down the steps.

The Executioner didn't wait for the dust and smoke to clear. He vaulted down the stairs three at a time. Reaching the landing, he dropped to one knee and opened up with the MAC-10. He sprayed the downed men at the foot of the stairs with a withering burst of 9 mm slugs. The bullets slapped flesh and sang off the patio's white flagstones. Savaged by multiple impacts, the bodies shuddered and jerked.

Then the mag came up empty.

Bolan jumped back to the stairs, out of the line of fire. As he did, a volley of bullets whined past him, thudding into the wall at the back of the landing. He heard the shouted order to resume the attack, then the tramp of more heavy feet coming his way. Unclipping two more M-429s from his harness, he pulled the pins and chucked them both at once, banking the plastic-bodied grenades off the landing's wall and down the steps. He dashed up the flight of stairs, again taking them three at a time. As he neared the top step, a deafening boom and rocking concussive blast slammed his back, nearly knocking him off his feet.

The Executioner took cover behind one of the upper story's concrete support posts. With his back to the post, he stripped the Ingram's empty magazine and rammed home a fresh one. After chambering a live round, he peered around the cover, looking over the balcony's rail. From his vantage point, he could see Murillo's men in the courtyard below. Some scrambled across the patio, others, still stunned or blinded, staggered or crawled away from the stairwell entrance. Before he could fire on them, they had reached the protection of the fountain or had moved under the balcony's overhang. On the other side of the pool, another target presented itself.

Roberto Murillo had grabbed the two boys and was pulling them away by the wrists.

Bolan shifted the MAC-10 to his left hand and unsheathed the 93-R from its holster. The Beretta was much more accurate than the submachine gun. With it, the Executioner was prepared to take a head shot at Murillo. The shot wasn't as challenging as it sounded. A relatively tall man was dragging away short kids. The range was far for the pistol.

For a man of Bolan's skills, it could be done.

As he led his target and started to tighten on the trigger, gunfire erupted from the balcony on the other side of the second floor. A half dozen slugs zinged into the support post above his head, forcing him to pull back behind it.

Before he withdrew, he got a glimpse of the shooters. Three men had taken position behind the balcony's rail in the middle of the suspended walkway. They were kneeling below the top rail and firing their semiautos from solid rests against the balusters. Their aimed fire continued to chew chunks of concrete out of the edge of the support post, pinning him down.

Bolan had no intention of staying pinned. Holstering his side arm, he pulled an M-68 impact fragmentation grenade from his harness. He yanked the pin and, stepping out from behind the post, high-arced the frag across the courtyard opening. The M-68 had an electrical fuze as well as a timed fuze. After a second or two of armed flight, the grenade's impact detonator was fully charged. He followed the M-68's flight for an instant, long enough to see that it was right on target.

Then he ducked back.

The grenade looped over the three men's heads and dropped behind them. When it hit the floor of the balcony, it detonated.

This explosion was different.

Not just louder.

This one screeched as fragments of red-hot steel sliced the air.

Bolan peered around the post. Amid a billowing cloud

of gray smoke, the entire midsection of the balcony broke free of the wall and tumbled onto the ground floor. All the windows on that side of the atrium had been blown out. Fire lapped at the shredded curtains and a great, semicircular, blackened area stained the wall.

The Murillo's rancho had gone from mansion to shambles in the space of four seconds.

In the courtyard, Roberto Murillo was in full retreat, protected by a phalanx of gunmen as he hauled the boys through the arched doorway that led to the rancho's front room.

Heavy-caliber autofire barked from widely spaced, second-floor positions on the other side of the atrium. The twin streams of sustained fire bracketing his cover made it instantly untenable, so Bolan abandoned it, diving through the open sliding door of the room behind him. The autorifles tracked his dive. A split second after he hit the floor inside, the glass door and window wall came apart, sending a hailstorm of sharp fragments sweeping over his back and head.

The gunfire only lasted a few seconds. When he looked up, he saw that the room wasn't empty.

In full-out firefights, shit happened—it was something the drug soldier on the floor by the closed hallway door had learned firsthand. He lay flat on his back, his torso ripped crosswise, from armpit to hip by 7.62 mm full-metal jackets. He wasn't dead, yet. His heels drummed on the tile floor.

Seeing his own guts spilled out on the floor was a hard thing.

A real hard thing.

As Bolan belly-crawled over the broken glass toward the door, the man begged him in Spanish for a mercy bullet, his voice shrill and desperate.

The Executioner granted his wish.

Another burst of automatic fire from the opposite balcony swept through the room, stitching a line of holes across the wall and door. When the shooting stopped, Bolan reached up from his position on the floor and gripped the door handle. Opening the door wide, he crawled forward and ducked his head around the bottom of the jamb. He checked the hallway in both directions. It looked clear, at least for the moment. Clear or not, he had to get to the front of the rancho before Murillo made his escape with the children. Bolan jumped to his feet.

As he launched himself through the doorway, more bullets sang through the room, plowing the interior wall and blistering the opposite side of the hallway. He sprinted down the corridor, away from the line of fire. His goal was at the far end, the flight of stairs leading down from the second story to the front room. The distance was short, no more than seventy-five feet. But just before the top of the staircase, the hallway took a left, winding around the front of the building.

A blind turn.

He was fifty feet away from his destination when three men stepped out from around the corner. Jockeying each other to get a clear angle, they opened up at once with their side arms. Three high-capacity autoloaders firing simultaneously produced a sizable quantity of lead. A maelstrom of it howled around him. Bullets cut into the floor, ceiling and walls.

There was no cover close to hand. No doorway he could duck into.

Dropping to one knee to make himself a smaller target, Bolan pinned the MAC-10's trigger, fanning the hall with Black Talon rounds.

Only one of the gunmen he faced had a decent position, with a clear shooting lane. But as that man fired, he closed his eyes.

If the bullets Murillo's soldiers sent his way went wide of their intended target, the Executioner's answering fire did not. It was right on the money. Under the MAC-10's merciless hail, the opposition clustered before him melted away, their bodies twisting, knees buckling, jolted by the howling rain of slugs he poured into them. They collapsed across the floor of the corridor and lay strewed there in a tangled heap.

Despite the slugs whining down the hallway inches from his head, the Executioner paused inside the doorway. He ripped open one of the ballistic nylon pouches on his belt and took out a prerigged explosive charge the size of a transistor radio. He tapped a forty-five-second delay into the detonator's LCD display and hit the arming switch. As the numbers on the display started to fall, he slapped the charge just outside the jamb, near the floor. He slammed the door and slid the lock's bolt closed.

When Bolan turned, out of the corner of his eye he caught the blur of a figure dashing across the room. Instinctively, he swung up the MAC-10, tracking the target as it moved rapidly out of the open bathroom door, across the rumpled queen-size bed and then dived between the mattresses and the wall. He held his fire.

The dark-haired young woman had been naked except for a short, pastel-pink negligee.

"Quickly, now," he said, as he advanced on the bed. "Show me your hands. Show me they're empty."

Huddled as far back in the corner as she could get, the girl held up her open palms. Behind the splayed fingers, her brown eyes were huge with fear.

"Get under the bed," he told her. "If you want to live, get under the bed and stay there."

Twenty-five seconds.

The Executioner stripped out the Ingram's clip. It had one bullet left. He discarded it and inserted another full magazine. A glance at his harness told him his ammo supply for the SMG was half used up. And he still had a long way to go.

He could hear footfalls coming up the hall. He rushed toward the curtains that covered the sliding-glass door.

His escape route was blocked.

If he stepped out on the balcony, Bolan knew he'd be sandwiched by autofire, with nowhere to go. If he exited the room that way, his only option would be to vault straight over the rail and drop the twenty feet to the ground floor. And in the process, perhaps twist an ankle or break a leg when he landed.

Fifteen seconds.

Then, the choice of how he wanted to die was taken out of his hands.

Automatic gunfire from the hallway slashed through the intervening wall. Bullets blasted divots in the plaster, paintings dropped from their hooks, vases exploded, the room's small table and two chairs ripped into splinters. Bolan hit the deck.

The Murillo gunmen were hoping to get lucky by saturating the room. They were way too busy to notice the surprise he had left for them outside the door.

Somebody shouted and the autofire ceased. As a boot slammed the hallway door, the Executioner crawled for the room's heavy couch, which stood against a side wall. As he squirmed in behind it feetfirst, he saw someone easing open the sliding door.

Time's up.

Bolan clamped his hands over his ears, opened his mouth and yelled as loud as he could, bellowing to equalize the pressure on his eardrums and keep from being deafened.

The C-4 exploded with such horrific force that it made Bolan black out for an instant. The blast's shock wave lifted the couch from the floor, smashing it and him against the wall. As the couch bounced away, the Sheetrock sloughed off the wall and fell on top of him.

Because he was behind the couch and momentarily unconscious, he didn't see the heavy hallway door blown free of its hinges, hurled sideways across the room and out through the glass wall.

Pushing up from under the chunks of rubble, the Executioner peered over the back of the couch, through the boiling pall of smoke and plaster dust and saw the devastation he had just wrought. The glass door and floor-to-ceiling windows and curtains had vanished, as had the balcony railing. The room was now completely open to the air. Piles of debris, shattered joists and wall studs, plates of fractured Sheetrock blocked the corridor.

For long seconds, there was an eerie silence. The inside of Bolan's head felt as if it was stuffed with cotton. He dragged himself out from behind the couch.

One look told him that the men in the hallway were buried under the fallen ceiling and timbers. Here and there, a blood-misted hand or foot stuck out of the rubble. The drug soldiers on the balcony outside had been swept away by the flying door, bowled along with it through the railing and out into space.

One end of the queen-size bed smoldered, and its mattresses hung off the edge of the frame, the fitted sheet and quilted top plundered and ripped by flying debris. Bolan knelt and checked under the bed.

It hadn't been such a great hiding place, after all.

Between the tile floor and the bottom of the box springs, the woman's face rested on her chin and left cheek. From the eyebrows down, her face was a mass of slowly oozing red. The door's iron bolt had been driven by the blast sideways through her forehead. The knob end of the little bar stuck out of her right temple.

The weighty silence that hung over ground zero came to an end. From the hallway just outside the room the soldier heard moans. Moans that quickly turned to screams. Bolan straightened and moved to the corridor.

The shrill cries came from under a pile of rubble. The Executioner shifted his submachine gun to his left hand,

and with the other lifted the chunks of Sheetrock and lumber, uncovering the face of one of Murillo's men, which was dusted with plaster and bled profusely from a scalp wound above the right ear.

The drug soldier blinked up at him, his gratitude turning to shock as he realized who was looking down at him. He opened his mouth to scream some more, but Bolan shook his head.

A fallen ceiling joist had the guy's legs pinned to the floor. Bolan cleared the obstacle, then, with the muzzle of the Ingram tucked tightly under the man's chin, he jerked him to his feet.

The guy didn't make a sound.

Except for the blood sheeting down the side of his face, over his ear and off his jawline, the soldier looked okay.

"Turn," Bolan said, gripping the man's shoulder and twisting him around. With a forearm locked across the front of the guy's throat and the MAC-10 jammed hard against his skull, the Executioner muscled the Murillo soldier down the hallway.

When they came to the dogleg where the corridor turned left around the front of the building, Bolan shoved the drug thug out in front of him into the hallway.

No one shot him.

A peek around the corner told Bolan it was safe to cross the corridor. He prodded the soldier with the muzzle of the MAC-10, forcing him to step up to the top of the flight of stairs. Again, this was not met with a flurry of gunfire. Down to the landing, the stairs were clear.

Bolan could read the guy's mind. It was shouting, "Jump! Jump, now!"

"If you move, I will kill you," he warned as he unclipped the last Thunderflash from his harness. He pulled the pin with his teeth, but held the grip safety in place.

"We're going down," Bolan said, giving the guy another shove. "Tell your amigos not to shoot. Tell them that you've killed the intruders, that everything's under control. And be convincing."

15

The American expatriates of San Bartolomeo cove shared a common philosophy. They all believed that *pace* was the key to full and proper boozifying. This involved sustaining a measured alcohol intake over many hours. Because of their training and dedication, Chip, Edwards, Ryan and Carlson were able to drink steadily from daybreak until nine or ten at night before their speech started to get slurred. Shortly after the mush mouth set in, like clockwork, like dominoes falling, they all passed out.

Their daily regimen began with a four-ounce, straight tequila eye-opener at sunrise, after which came a leisurely and prolonged breakfast of ice-cold Pacifico beer. Maybe six bottles spread out over three or four hours. After their solitary breakfasts and halfhearted toilets, they came together, either in the shade of their porches or the palm grove, and shared Mexican rice paper cigarettes and home-grown bullshit while sipping at insulated mugs of nearly frozen Oso Negro. Lunch consisted of another six-pack of Pacifico, again stretched over several hours.

It was the consensus among the expats at San Bartolomeo that Pacifico had more nutrition than Oso Negro, although the facts behind this assumption had never been directly tested.

After lunch came more tequila sipping. The really serious, let-your-hair-down, recreational drinking didn't start until after dinner.

When Chip, Edwards, Ryan and Carlson heard the first gun-crack that afternoon, they were sitting in the shade of the palm trees in their lawn chairs, just finishing up the last swallows of their lunch.

Chip cocked his head toward the sound and frowned. "Long gun," he said, pleased that he had got out his analysis before any of the others.

Gunfire wasn't a rare occurrence at the Murillo rancho. Their patrons' bodyguards often took target practice up on the plain, using the low hills as backstops. And this time of year, the gringo big-game hunters up in the Sierra de la Gigante were blasting away at mountain sheep.

There was a placidity, a serenity to the daily lives of these men. Lives punctuated and measured by emptied brown bottles and two-quart plastic jugs. Though their backgrounds were very different, though they each drank for different reasons, for all of them the rancho was a refuge. A monastery for boozers. A place where a man could live for free and drink himself to sleep every night.

Chip and Ryan were both ex-military. The older man had burned out in Vietnam, thirty years before; Ryan had come to the end of his fuse in Desert Storm. Edwards was a former Los Angeles cop who lost his badge because of his beverage-related hobby. Carlson was the only former entrepreneur. He had owned a gun shop in Pacoima, California, until a bitter divorce had cost him the business and most of his self-respect. He'd gone from being a recreational drinker to a full-time professional in a matter of a months. All four of them had been wandering aimlessly south of the border when they happened upon San Bartolomeo. It took a certain kind of dedication to cross the twenty miles of hell to get here. And by the time a guy arrived, he was mighty thirsty.

None of them cared about money. Which was good because the Murillos didn't pay them. What they got was free room and board. And once a day, a Jeep came down from the rancho to restock their beer and tequila stores.

They knew who the Murillos were, how they made and kept their fortunes and they didn't care.

The expats had no sense of shame.

And no ambition. It didn't matter that there was nothing to do and no one to do it with.

So long as the liquor kept on flowing on the house.

Then the second and third rifle shots rang out in close succession. The echoes were confused, indistinct.

"Where're those goddamned shots coming from?" Edwards said, lowering his insulated mug. "I can't seem to source them."

"Up in the Sierra," Ryan said.

"No fucking way," Chip countered. "They're coming from the plain, up behind the rancho."

"Sound kind of funny to me," Carlson commented without much enthusiasm. He had his eyes shut, his head was tipped back and he held his mug in resting position in the middle of his big belly.

Chip pushed out of his lawn chair. He'd been sitting in one position for too long. He walked stiffly toward the rusty wheelbarrow that held a sixty-gallon plastic cooler. He lifted the lid and saw that the ice inside had long since melted. The yellow-and-red labels had come off the submerged brown bottles. "Anybody want another beer?"

Silly question.

A little later, the sound of a Thunderflash grenade exploding made the little no-name dog at their feet jolt upright, wide awake, his long, pointed ears stiffly erect. He looked over his purple-scarred shoulder at the bluff, in the direction of the rancho and whimpered softly.

"What the hell was that?" Carlson said, lumbering out of his lawn chair.

"Sounded like a bomb to me," Edwards said.

"Ain't no bombs up there," Ryan said.

They all looked at Chip, who was frowning.

Before Chip could throw in his two cents, small-arms fire crackled from the plain. Volleys of it. It didn't sound like the usual, halfhearted target practice the Mexicans indulged in. There were too many guns going off at once—it was never that well organized. And the shooting continued, sawing back and forth as gunfire answered gunfire.

On the rim of the cove, the sniper had risen from his hide and was waving frantically at them and pointing across the plain at the rancho.

"I don't like the looks of that," Edwards said, squinting into the sun.

"We got us some real trouble," Chip exclaimed as he hopped out of his chair. "That's a fucking firefight!"

The words were barely out of his mouth when the second pair of Thunderflashes detonated. At the sound, the little dog took off. Head lowered, ears back, tail tucked between his legs, he shot through the palm trees in the direction of San Nicolas.

"Get your goddamned gear, this isn't a drill. Let's saddle up!" Ryan said.

The expats dropped the beer bottles and raced for their waterfront houses. In a few seconds they reappeared on their porches with flat-black automatic rifles and backpacks full of extra, loaded magazines. Chip took the lead, waving for them to follow him around the curve of the beach. The others shoulder-slung their M-16s and double-timed it up the dirt road after him, making for the battered GMC pickup truck that was parked in the shade on the other side of the wooden gate.

Though their destination was only a few hundred yards away up a very slight grade, by the time they arrived their faces were flushed crimson from the blistering heat, the sudden exertion and their excitement.

Gunfire still rattled from the plain above as Edwards and

Ryan piled into the pickup's bed. Chip got behind the wheel and Carlson climbed in through the passenger's door.

"Come on, baby, come on," Chip said as he turned the ignition key. He revved it hard and dropped the truck into first gear. When he popped the clutch, the rear wheels spun momentarily in the soft dirt, then caught. The GMC lurched violently forward and sideways. Chip cut the wheel over and mashed the gas pedal to the floorboard, powering out of the skid.

"Hang on, you bastards!" he shouted out the window as engine roaring, the truck shot up the winding road.

16

"It's over, Patron," a shaky voice called down the stairwell to the first floor. "We got them all. We killed the fuckers. It's me, Raimundo Ortega. Don't shoot, it's Raimundo."

Roberto Murillo's men turned to their leader for orders, relief evident on all their faces.

Murillo felt very little relief, himself. His dominant emotion at that instant was fury. He stood next to the arched doorway leading out to the atrium. He could see his lovely swimming pool desecrated with a logjam of jagged debris. Smoke from the fires burning in the second-floor rooms hung over the courtyard in an eye-stinging, swirling, gray haze. Whoever had destroyed his beautiful rancho had done so in the span of a few minutes, had done so almost matter-of-factly.

Even if the attackers were dead now, as far as he was concerned it was too little too late. Murillo was anything but pleased with the performance of his soldiers. From the way they had been steamrollered, it appeared that their training had been wholly inadequate. Training that he, himself, had organized and implemented down to the smallest detail. Of course, every field general knows that no amount of training can turn a coward into a hero. But field generals rarely have the luxury of hand-selecting their troops, as Murillo had. Which brought him back to the same unpleasant conclusion, that what had happened to the rancho had been in part at least his fault.

He raised the Smith & Wesson semiauto pistol in a two-handed grip, taking aim at the archway across the room that opened onto the bottom of the stairs.

No verbal orders were necessary.

No hand signal was required.

The men would follow Murillo's lead. If he opened up on the person who appeared on the stairs, they had the green light to fire as well.

Murillo glanced over his shoulder at the boys huddled at the very back of the great fireplace. Their eyes were downcast, their heads averted from the action. So soft, Murillo thought. Soft like little girls. Too much mama. Too little papa.

As he turned back to the pistol's sights, he recalled the first time he had ever seen a man killed. He'd been about Juanito's age. It had been a stabbing. Four on one in a vacant lot near the tumbledown shack where he and Ramon were living at the time. What had amazed him was the power of the blows the assailants struck. They slammed their knives into the defenseless man's torso, over and over.

The man getting stabbed to death had been his uncle Tomas, who had stolen the wrong man's drugs.

Young Roberto hadn't looked away once.

Slow, careful footsteps descended the staircase. "I'm coming down, now," said the voice from above.

Murillo didn't recognize it as belonging to Raimundo Ortega. The voice was so hoarse, it could have been anyone.

"Do it very slowly," Murillo warned as he thumbed back the autopistol's exposed hammer. The first shot from the 9 mm would be single action. Quick and steady. Murillo growled over his shoulder to the man guarding the foot of the opposite staircase, "Keep watch on the steps on your side. This might be a trick."

The soldier nodded and turned.

Just below the top of the arch and above the sights of

Murillo's pistol, a pair of feet appeared on the stairs. The feet weren't clad in shoes, but rather, in dark-blue dress socks. As the feet stepped down cautiously, legs and dusty trousers torn at both knees came into view.

"Don't stop!" Murillo shouted.

When he saw the man's empty hands hanging at his sides, he said, "Hands on top of your head!"

The man obeyed as he continued to descend. His face appeared, bloodied and pale. Eyes full of terror.

"It's Raimundo!" the guard behind the bar said, allowing the sights of his M-16 to drop. "It's Raimundo Ortega!"

Ortega was scared. Absolutely petrified. This despite the fact that he had been recognized by his compadres.

Which told Murillo that the man wasn't scared of what was in front of him, but what was behind. Before he could shout a warning to his soldiers, something small and dark thunked down the stairs between Ortega's legs. It landed at the bottom of the steps. Hissing.

In the two seconds that it took for the Thunderflash to explode, Murillo fired six times as fast as he could squeeze the S&W's trigger, nailing his own man in the middle of his chest. This wasn't payback for Ortega's betrayal so much as a warning to whoever was hidden up the stairs behind him. A warning that death awaited.

Ortega's knees started to cave. Then everything went white.

Murillo reacted by shutting his eyes, tight.

The stun grenade's flash was so bright, this had little effect. Eyelids were no protection from the blast of light. It felt as though someone had thrust dull pencils deep into Murillo's eye sockets. He had no time to contemplate the agonizing sensation. A fraction of a second later, the resounding thunderclap slammed him against the courtyard doorway and dropped him to the floor on his hands and knees.

Blinded and deafened, Roberto Murillo knew what would come next: a full-out assault on the helplessly stunned. Kill at will. He raised his autopistol and opened fire with only the vaguest notion of where he was shooting. Where didn't matter. He was just trying to put up a defense, any defense. He fired another nine rounds in rapid succession, hardly able to hear his own gunshots. He squeezed the trigger until the pistol's slide locked back empty.

Other weapons cut loose from the other side of the room. The full-auto bursts sounded muffled and distant.

Murillo's eyes recovered before his ears, a fog lifting. In front of him, things were happening at light speed.

A single enemy moved away from the bottom of the stairs, gliding through the gunsmoke in a blur. The gringo was tall and had camouflage paint on his face; his expression was hard and confident. The muzzle of the SMG in his hands flamed a strobing star burst as he walked autofire across the front of the leather couch. Several 9 mm slugs whapped against the tanned skin, kicking out great tufts of white stuffing as they passed through the back of the couch. The soldier crouching behind the sofa took multiple hits to his chest and face and slumped to the floor on his side.

Kill him! Murillo thought. In the searing heat of the moment he was unable to make his lips form the shout. Kill him!

Of course, his men were trying to do just that.

The guy behind the bar had shouldered his M-16 and was streaming rounds toward the rapidly moving target, in the process chewing up the walls and the furniture. Before he could make the line of slugs catch up, the tall guy had him bracketed. As the front edge of the bar disintegrated in a flurry of splinters, so did the soldier, his arms flying wide. An instant before he dropped out of sight, his forehead exploded.

The guy in the opposite stairwell was trying to shoot through his mortally wounded partner to hit the intruder.

It didn't work.

As the man fell behind the bar, the war-painted assassin shifted his aim slightly. Full-automatic fire stitched the other drug soldier from crotch to chin. The impacts made him stagger backward. As he fell onto the stairs, he convulsed, emptying his magazine into the ceiling.

The soldier standing beside Murillo had seen enough. He turned and lunged headlong for the exit.

Murillo had to move in that direction as well or be knocked down. As he stepped through the doorway, his soldier was right on his heels, actually brushing against him as a stream of bullets hammered the archway. Something sharp hit Murillo solidly in the back of the head. Then a heavy weight came down on his legs, tripping him, sending him crashing across the threshold on his face. The weight slammed on top of his legs. Dead weight pinned him to the floor.

He cranked his head around and saw a red crater where the face of the drug soldier had been.

For a second Murillo, in his panic, almost scrambled out from under the twitching corpse. But then he thought better of it.

The weapon he still clutched in his hand was empty. Cover was a long way off and the man who had so easily slaughtered his crew no more than twenty feet away. To try and run was suicide.

Execution.

A gooey wetness trickled down the sides of his neck. Murillo put his face to the white stone flagging and lay very still, breathing in the tiniest of breaths. He heard the heavy crunch of a boot from behind. And in that terrible instant he was sure the intruder knew he was alive and was about to give him a coup de grâce.

He awaited sudden death with every muscle tensed and his teeth clenched.

WHEN THE EXPLOSION ripped the floor above, its concussion shook the fireplace's walls, raining soot on the two boys huddled in back of the log grate.

Juanito looked into his little brother's eyes and saw the fear that reflected his own. They had no mother or father to protect them. It was the same utter helplessness Juanito had felt the day before in the Tijuana safehouse when it was attacked. Only this time, the destruction was far more terrible.

What chance did he and Pedro have?

The violence of the explosion set his knees trembling. As much as he was covering, shielding his brother's body with his, Pedro was supporting him. They hugged each other so tightly they could hardly breathe.

When the shooting and explosions stopped after a minute or two, Pedro whispered, "Is it over?"

Juanito looked up and out of the fireplace, brushing the soot from his eyes.

"Is it over?" Pedro pleaded.

In his heart, Juanito knew it wasn't. The monster that stalked them was immortal. It could never be killed.

When the man called down from the staircase, saying the enemy was dead, he knew it was a lie. There was something in the man's voice. A shakiness. It told Juanito that the soldier was even more scared than Pedro. He shouldn't have been scared if it was really all over.

Juanito thought Roberto must've realized this, too. Because he pointed his gun at the stairs. Then the other guards did the same.

The boy knew that whoever was coming down the steps was going to die.

Having seen so many dead men in the Tijuana mansion, Juanito had no desire to see more. He turned his face away and pushed his little brother against the back wall of the fireplace, shoving him lower behind the huge iron grate.

When the shooting started, a rapid string of single pistol shots, Juanito flinched.

Then the whole room rocked.

For an instant, there were no shadows. Not even in the back of the fireplace. The loud noise felt like giant palms clapping against the sides of his head. More soot and small chunks of mortar tumbled down on top of him. Pedro slipped to the ground.

The monster still lived.

Though his ears were ringing and useless, Juanito could feel the impacts of the bullets through the soles of his feet. They slammed into the furniture and walls as the full-auto gun battle raged. Dropping to his knees, he covered his brother's body. He shut his eyes tightly and withdrew into himself as deeply as he could, curling up like a pill bug.

When a big hand touched his back, he jerked violently away. Juanito wasn't even aware that the shooting had stopped. Looking up, he saw a face daubed with stripes of brown and black and eyes the color of blue ice. In his other hand, the man held a gun, the muzzle of which still smoked.

Was this the monster?

Juanito wanted to say, "Don't kill us." He opened his mouth to speak but no sound came out.

"I'm not here to hurt you," the tall man said. He had a deep voice and it was very calm. Not cold. Calm. "My name is Striker. Your mother sent me. She asked me to bring you back to her."

Pedro stood, his grimy cheeks streaked with tears. "I want my mama," he moaned.

"Come with me," Striker said.

Juanito could see the bodies strewed around the room, the blackened ceiling and walls. He could smell the smoke from fires burning upstairs. Despite that, this man was asking them to trust him. He was asking when, of course, they had no choice in the matter. He had the gun, he could make them go with him. Oddly though, Juanito did trust him.

Instinctively and completely. A boy of eight still lives in his heart, not his mind. In this man's care, he knew that he and his little brother would come to no harm. He took hold of Pedro's hand and led his brother out of the fireplace.

In the distance, they heard the sound of a car honking its horn.

More of the Murillos's guards?

"I want you to follow close behind me," the tall man said. "And do exactly what I say. We're getting out of here."

Striker led them through a doorway, down a short hall and into the rancho's kitchen. The food service staff had long since hightailed it; the place was deserted, big pots left simmering on the stove, water running in the sinks. The door to the outside had been left wide open.

Bolan peered around the doorway, then said, "Stay to my right."

The three of them ran across the open space, heading for the break in the masonry wall near the vehicle storage area. When they were twenty feet from the opening, gunfire erupted from the front of the rancho, sparking off the wall ahead of them.

Striker used his body to shield the boys. Shifting the gun to his left hand, he returned fire in a wide spray.

"Run!" he said. "Run!"

17

The barren hillsides of Tijuana's outskirts rolled past the Mercedes stretch limousine's one-way, black-tinted glass. Ramon Murillo stared dispassionately at the passing scene.

Driving over the cobblestone road caused an unpleasant, steady vibration to rumble through the heavy car's frame. There were no gutters or drainage ditches framing the road—no water, power or telephone lines. As the Mercedes climbed the grade, the cobblestones disappeared, and the road became all dirt. The houses got even smaller and simpler.

In a swirling cloud of yellow dust, Murillo's driver pulled over to the side of the road, below an unpainted, one-room, hillside shack made of scraps of plywood. A blue-and-white striped blanket hung over the lone doorway on a piece of clothesline cord. The crudely sawed windows had neither glass nor fabric covering them. Half buried tires formed a retaining wall that kept the shack from sliding down the slope and onto the road.

It was in such a hovel that Ramon Murillo and his brother grew up.

The man nicknamed Three Nails got out of the limo and started up the narrow footpath to the hut. As he climbed, a pair of small, yellow-and-white dogs rushed at him out of nowhere, barking and showing their teeth. He ignored them.

A corner of the blanket covering the doorway pulled back a crack, then swung aside. Standing on the threshold was an extremely short woman with steely gray hair drawn into a tight bun. She wore a shapeless, badly faded, print dress and terry cloth slippers. She beamed a broad smile at him; it was gap-toothed, top and bottom.

"Good afternoon," he said.

"Good afternoon, Don Ramon. Have you come to visit me? Please come in out of the sun." She stepped to one side and held open the blanket for him to enter.

As he passed by her, he could hear her labored breathing. Wet. Bubbling. Gasping. And yet her sweet smile didn't waver.

The shack had a pounded dirt floor. A single window had been cut in the plywood that formed the rear wall. A piece of clear plastic had been nailed over the hole. It was a dark little place, but spotlessly clean. There was a single pallet in the corner, raised off the floor a few inches by concrete blocks; for a dresser, a cardboard box. The sink was a corrugated metal washtub, while the combination woodstove and cooker was a recycled steel drum that vented through a pipe to the roof. The hut's other furniture consisted of a small metal card table and one folding metal chair.

The old woman dusted off the seat of the chair with a rag and bade him sit.

After he had done so, she perched herself on the edge of the pallet.

The only decorations on the walls were three pictures. None of the frames had glass in them. One was a painting of Jesus, one was a photograph of a large family with many small children and the third was of a teenage boy. The frame of the latter was garlanded with black crepe and dried flowers.

"How are you feeling?" Murillo asked her.

From the light of the doorway, the seams in her face looked like thousands of fine scars. "I'm very near the end,

I think," she told him. She looked at the boy's black-draped photo. "Soon I'll see my Carlos again."

The color photograph had been taken years ago, when her son had been in high school.

"How's his family doing?"

"Well enough, thanks to your generosity. And that of your brother, Don Roberto."

"I have a proposition to make you," Murillo said. "I came to you first with it, because I know the condition of your health and because of Carlos's sacrifice."

"I have always appreciated your thoughtfulness to me, Don Ramon. What is the proposition?"

Murillo leaned forward on the hard chair. The old woman's son, Carlos, a longtime enforcer for the Murillo organization, had been killed in the line of duty while protecting his employer. Five months earlier, an up-and-coming rival Baja gang had sent its hitmen to take out Murillo as he returned from an oceanview restaurant he favored. They had set up an ambush along the coastal highway with roadblocks.

Murillo, his driver and his bodyguards had to bail out of the limo and fight toe-to-toe for their lives. With everyone shooting at once, hundreds of rounds were expended in a matter of seconds. In the chaos, Murillo and his crew got outflanked by a pair of rival gunmen. At the last instant, Carlos had stepped in front of his boss and taken a dozen machine gun bullets intended for Murillo. He left a wife and five young children. As Carlos's Patrons, it was expected that the Murillos do something to take care of the family. They chose to maintain them in the life-style their dead husband and father had provided while he was alive. What Ramon Murillo was now offering was something more. In return for another, similar sacrifice.

When he explained to the old woman what needed to be done, her eyes widened. When he explained what the reward would be, tears began streaming down her face. She got up, took his hand in her leathery fingers and kissed his knuckles. She only had one question of him: "When, Don Ramon?"

He rose from the chair. "You must come with me now."

The old woman wiped away her tears with her dust rag.

Murillo waited patiently by the doorway, holding aside the blanket while she took down and tenderly kissed the portraits of Jesus and her son, then rehung them.

Outside her shack, the old woman paused for a last look to the north. With shining eyes, she looked past the sprawling jumble of the Tijuana basin. Through the haze of wood smoke and factory and car exhaust, she could see the gridwork streets of Chula Vista, with the new, upscale residential developments on the far side of the border.

Fine big houses.

Paved roads.

Good schools.

Endless opportunities.

It would all be her gift to her grandchildren. A magnificent gift to the future.

She turned toward Murillo and he nodded solemnly.

With ten million dollars, everything was possible.

UNDER THE TABLE, Yovana Ortiz's hands trembled uncontrollably on her lap. Time ticked by as she awaited word of her children. Two hours seemed like forever when she was counting every tick of the clock.

She waited in silence, half suffocated by dread and self-doubt. She asked herself over and over if she had done the right thing by going to the Feds in the first place. Or had it been a terrible blunder? Though she was trying to protect her boys, though she was willing to give up everything she had to achieve that end, she had only succeeded in putting them in mortal danger. If the tall man from the El Zorro Azul failed to rescue her children, if the Murillos turned them over to Samosa, she knew she would never see them again, whether she lived or died.

"Can I get you another soft drink, some coffee or something to eat?" the big Fed asked her. "There's a bar upstairs, if you want me to bring you something stronger."

The man sitting on the other side of the conference table had eyes that could penetrate and read a person's very soul. Sad eyes that had seen many bad things. Sad, but not soft.

"No, thank you," she said. Ortiz made a point of always looking him straight in the face when she spoke to him. She knew if she didn't meet his gaze, he would suspect that she was holding back. Of course, she was withholding something.

Something important.

Though the romantic connection between Ortiz and Don Jorge Samosa was widely known, she had managed to keep secret the fact that he was the father of her two children. After she had become pregnant with Juanito, she had helped to spread a fictitious story about an ongoing relationship with a much older costar on one of the Mexican soap operas. Because the May-December story was sexy and romantic, everybody in the press had bought into it. The male star in question never denied the allegations. They helped to quell long-standing rumors about his offstage virility.

Both Ortiz and Samosa had agreed that the secrecy was a necessity—only a few of his most trusted associates, like the Murillos, knew the truth. Samosa had far too many enemies. The children of an international drug lord would be under constant threat of kidnapping, or even murder, by other drug lords and by foreign governments. Once they were identified as the sons of Samosa, Juanito and Pedro could never hope to have a normal life. Ortiz and Samosa had agreed that a normal life meant they would reside with their mother ninety percent of the time.

Though her goals for her children remained the same,

Samosa's attitude had changed of late. He had begun to demand more control over them and he had told her that he wanted them to take over his empire someday. Because of this, Ortiz had been forced into action. The last thing she wanted for her boys was to have them follow in their father's bloody footsteps.

She didn't know why he'd changed his mind about keeping the boys out of the drug trade. Except that he was getting older, approaching fifty. Perhaps he was starting to think about his own mortality. Perhaps he'd had some health crisis that he'd kept from her. Perhaps he didn't want to see his illicit empire, his monument crumble—or be torn apart by ten thousand jackals—after his death.

Even though Samosa had ordered her murder, she still had strong feelings for him. She loved and hated the man in almost equal measure. How could she be a real, flesh-and-blood woman and not find herself torn between those conflicting emotions? After all, Ortiz, now pushing thirty, had given up her youth to the shadowy drug lord, and despite knowing all his terrible faults, had borne him two sons. Though he had the reputation of being a ruthless criminal monster, a reputation he more than deserved, time and again she had witnessed Samosa's great tenderness to her and their children. He had been present for their births. And when he was with his boys he was truly with them, protecting, nurturing, playfully challenging them.

Had she known who he really was when they had first met she would have never gotten involved with him. Samosa had presented himself as a Latin-American businessman, an extremely wealthy businessman. He was confident, even arrogant, and he had the kind of rugged, masculine good looks that could turn a woman's head. From the start between them it had been a matter of chemistry; and for her, chemistry quickly became a matter of the heart. Ortiz didn't consciously decide to go with the biggest, boldest, richest man she could find. It had just worked out that way.

Only after they'd become lovers did Samosa reveal the source of his wealth to her. He told her he'd had to keep his identity a secret because of the constant danger of assassination. He said that he was telling her his secret because he trusted her with his life. By the time she learned this, Ortiz was too much in love to make a rational judgment.

Those feelings persisted, even though he made no bones about being faithful to her. When she was absent, which was most of the time, he regularly cycled other women in and out of his life. Ortiz had been forced to accept this, her consolation being that she was still number one, the woman he kept coming back to. To prove her own, continuing devotion, she had agreed to do certain things for her lover, illegal things.

Things she now deeply regretted.

Though Samosa was willing to kill her, indeed, wanted her dead for betraying him, she wished him no such fate. It wasn't in her character to wish for a loved one's death. Nor would she ever knowingly act in a way to cause it.

She was determined not to give up all the incriminating information she had, information that had the power to bring Samosa down. The loss of the Mexican arm of his operation might sorely sting, but it wouldn't be fatal. At most, it would only be a temporary setback for him. Hurting the man she still loved was a necessity if she wanted to get her kids and herself away from him for good, but the consequences of that betrayal were limitless. Simply put, she had had no other option than to cooperate with the U.S. government, at least to a certain degree.

And having taken that precipitous step, she felt as if she had awakened from a deep and troubled sleep. She had awakened only to discover that reality was a perfect nightmare.

Ortiz checked the wall clock again. Three minutes had passed since she'd last looked.

"If there's anything else you want to talk about," the big Fed said, "anything at all, I'm a good listener."

Looking into the road map of his face, she believed that. And though she felt the urge to unburden herself, she knew he was a policeman, not a priest. Whatever she told him he would be free to act upon. Under the table, she dug her fingernails deep into the palms of her hands and said nothing.

18

Bullets stitched along the ground to Mack Bolan's left, kicking up puffs of dirt, then climbed the face of the stuccoed wall, gouging out a line of bright, white, quarter-size craters. Tiny flying fragments of plaster stung his face as he herded the boys through the gap to momentary safety.

"That way. Turn right," he told them. The Executioner ran at the children's heels, shielding them from the rear with his body as they sprinted along the outside of the wall toward the vehicle storage area.

When they arrived at the palm-roofed canopy, he waved them on. "Keep going," he said. "Get behind the cars." Turning, he raised the MAC-10 and sent a burst of 9 mm slugs back along the wall. The bullets clipped the area on both sides of the gap. There was no one to aim at. He just wanted to make the pursuers think twice before sticking their heads out.

It only kept them back for an instant.

Even as he turned to follow the boys, autofire rattled from behind and more slugs slapped the dirt around him, zinging off the garage's stucco. The M-89 sniper rifle was right where he had left it. As he passed, he picked up the weapon and slipped its sling over his shoulder. Catching up to the children, he steered them along the row of parked vehicles.

Bolan jerked open the rear left passenger's door of the dark-green Suburban. "Get in and get down on the floor," he said. "I want you to stay there until I tell you to get up. Understand?"

The younger boy couldn't respond. He was too scared.

"Do you understand?" Bolan repeated.

Juanito pushed his brother into the SUV, climbed in after him, then shoved him down behind the front seat.

The Executioner jumped in behind the wheel and, as he did so, he set the butt of the M-89 on the floor in front of the passenger's seat, tightly wedging the barrel and its Arconus suppressor against the door. The Ingram he laid across his lap, safety off.

The mission's plan A, which had been unlikely from the get go, was now out of the question. For plan A to have worked, Bolan would have had to eliminate every gun inside and outside the rancho compound. It was impossible given the setup and the mission's priority to take control of and protect the children. With multiple shooters still operational, and close at hand, Jack Grimaldi couldn't touch down at the rancho airstrip to pick up the kids. A couple of guys with autorifles could literally tear the single-engine plane apart. Which meant plan B was in effect. The mission's alternative put distance between the Executioner, his young charges and the rancho's soldiers, in order to give Grimaldi a window of opportunity for a quick landing and takeoff.

Before Bolan reached for the ignition, he snatched the remote control detonator out of its harness pouch and set it on the dashboard. Cranking up the big diesel, he shifted into four-wheel-drive and roared out from under the shade of the canopy, into the searing sunlight.

The Murillos's gunmen weren't far behind. He'd traveled no more than seventy-five feet when a flurry of slugs whacked the Suburban's rear doors. Because it was intended to carry the rancho's Patrons, the heavy vehicle was reinforced with bulletproof side panels, and all the glass was likewise armored. Even so, the multiple bullet impacts caused the rear glass to shatter.

Swerving to avoid more hits, over his shoulder to the boys he shouted, "Stay down!" The autofire stopped almost at once. As he sped across the airstrip, he glanced in his side mirror and saw the reason for the sudden cease-fire. The drug soldiers had stopped shooting in order to take up the chase. A pickup truck accelerated out from under the palm canopy, followed by the other Suburban and a second pickup.

The soldier held the accelerator flat and steered toward the hangar and the fuel dump. With the speedometer's needle creeping past eighty, the hangar and gas drums flashed by in a blur. Driving one-handed, he lifted the remote detonator from the dashboard and armed it with a flick of his thumb.

He kept the Suburban going straight, making the gunners think he was going to continue in that direction, forcing them to follow more or less in his tracks or lose ground. In the rearview mirror, the hangar grew rapidly smaller.

With the dust clouds his own vehicle was raising, it was difficult to judge precisely when the other vehicles were going to come up even with the fuel dump. They had all turned on their headlights to combat the flying dust, which helped a bit, though. Bolan made an educated guess and hit the detonator's switch.

The effect was instantaneous and cataclysmic.

Through the haze of dust, fire bloomed sideways, billowing orange and red, spilling over and engulfing the hangar in a heartbeat. Simultaneously, the shock wave of a tremendous explosion slammed the back of the Suburban. In the rearview mirror, Bolan saw the gasoline-fueled fireball shoot skyward, creating a dome of flame that covered a hundred yards of tarmac.

"GET THE BASTARD!" Roberto Murillo snarled at his men. "Don't let him get past the airstrip!"

The soldiers lowered their heads and charged through the opening. As the sniper rushed by with his scoped, Heckler & Koch G-3 SG/1 rifle, Murillo caught him by the arm and jerked him aside. "Not you, Drigo," he said. "In case we can't contain him inside the fence and he makes it to the road, I want you to take one of the ATVs. I want you to go cross-country over the hills and set up a killing ground there. If he breaks out of the compound, you've got to beat him to the other side of the mountains. Do you understand me?"

"What about the children, Patron?" asked Drigo Martinez. "When I start shooting they could be hurt or even killed."

"The boys must not be allowed to reach Highway 1," Murillo told the rifleman. "I don't care how you do it. I'll pay you half a million dollars if you stop them."

The man's eyes widened.

"But if you let them get past you and escape, Drigo," Murillo went on, "understand that I'll gut you myself and then leave you staked out for the buzzards."

Fully aware of the potential rewards and punishments, the sniper about-faced and ran for the ATV. Murillo continued on, following the charge to the rancho's garage. As he stepped under the canopy, his men were cutting loose on the rear of the speeding Suburban. Roberto Murillo raised his weapon and, along with others, barraged the back of the rapidly retreating SUV.

Seeing that the bullets were having no effect, he shouted over the din, "Hold your fire! Let's get after them!"

Murillo sent three of his men to one of the pickup trucks, four to another. As he jumped into the front passenger's seat of the remaining Suburban, five soldiers climbed in with him. By the time his driver got the heavy SUV started and moving, one of the pickups, the Chevy, had already roared out from under the canopy and was in hot pursuit. As the Suburban plowed through the swirling clouds of grit raised by the vehicles ahead, visibility dropped.

The driver switched on his high beams.

"Faster!" Murillo said. "Don't let them out of sight!"

It occurred to him then that given what was at stake, some extra insurance was in order. He snatched up the satellite phone from its console cradle and punched a nine-digit code into its keypad. In the distance, he could just make out the rear of the fleeing Suburban. It was already past the hangar and heading off-road due west.

The man who answered on the second ring was an off-duty policeman on the Murillo payroll. After identifying himself, Murillo said, "Chuey, I need you to set up a road-block at the south end of Bahia Concepción. I want two cruisers at the Highway 1 turnoff to the San Bartolomeo road. You're looking for a dark-green Suburban. The driver is an assassin. He just hit the rancho. Don't try to arrest him. Just shoot him." Anticipating the man's question, he added, "If you kill him for me, Chuey, you'll never have to work again. That I promise you."

Murillo reached over to replace the phone in its cradle. As he did, they sped by the aircraft hangar. And then all hell broke loose.

The impact of the explosion was like being broadsided by a freight train. The shock wave slammed the Suburban, tipping it up on its left wheels, almost flipping it on its side. Roberto Murillo's head slammed into the passenger's window, and at the same instant, flame swept across the windshield, enveloping the vehicle. A wall of infernal, paint-blistering heat hit the side of his face that was turned toward the glass. The blast was so intense, so extreme, that for a split second it felt ice-cold.

BOLAN TAPPED his brakes and cut a sweeping left turn, heading south across the plain toward the gate in the steel fence. He didn't look behind him. There wasn't time. A half mile ahead the steel gate was still wide open; it hadn't been closed after the pickup truck from the cove had passed through. Two men hurried from the guardhouse to try to shut it before he got there. The Executioner put the hammer down.

As he stomped the accelerator, he reached across his chest to the left strap of his combat harness. His fingers found the transmit button of the palm-size, VHF minitransceiver he wore clipped there. The communications channel between the mission's assault and extraction units had been preset.

"Blackjack," he said, "this is Striker. Do you copy?"

When he released the transmit button, the tiny speaker let out a hiss of static.

The Executioner hit the button again and repeated the call.

This time, amid the static there was a response. "Blackjack, here," Jack Grimaldi said. "Striker, you're breaking up bad."

"I'm en route to Beta in a dark-green Suburban. Do you copy?"

"Roger, I copy that, Striker. Beta, it is. And your ride is a dark-green Suburban. My ETA is twenty-three minutes. I'll circle until I have visual on you. Blackjack out."

Bolan put both hands on the steering wheel. He was rapidly closing on the gate, which the sentries had managed to push shut. One of the men had slipped around to the far side, while the other guy was trying to wrap a chain around the gatepost. The first sentry used the gate's rails to brace himself and opened fire with an autorifle, blistering bullet holes across the SUV's armored windshield.

The glass chipped, but kept out the slugs, some of which flattened and stuck in the windshield.

Without slowing, Bolan steered for the gatepost. The guy fumbling with the chain looked up at the last second. From the stunned expression on his face, he realized that he wasn't going to make it. It was already too late to jump aside. The Suburban's left front fender clipped him, sending his body cartwheeling backward through the air. The bumper hit the unlocked end of the gate, crashing it open. The sentry standing on the other side was slammed by the gate as it snapped off its hinges. Both he and the gate went flying.

As Bolan roared on, the way ahead clear, he glanced into the rearview mirror. Through the billowing dust, he could see two bright pinpoints of yellow light.

High beams.

The fuel dump explosion hadn't taken out all of the pursuit.

Keeping the accelerator pinned, the Executioner followed the rutted track down into the San Bartolomeo canyon. As he neared the bottom of the grade, he feathered the brakes, slowing to make the turn that was coming up. The road west, toward Bahia Concepción and the highway, took the route of least resistance, following the seasonal stream channels that wound around the eroded hills and ridges.

When he hit the junction, he turned right. Instead of the long straightaways and open vistas of the plain, he faced a one-lane dirt road that curved sharply every thirty or forty yards. Stunted scrub trees and stands of tall, reedlike grass made every turn a blind corner. There were sheer cliff walls on both sides.

"Okay, boys," he said over the seat's back as he slewed the Suburban through the first set of turns. "I want you both to get off the floor, now. Sit on the seat and buckle your safety belts nice and tight." In the rearview mirror, he could see the tops of their heads as they did as he asked. When he looked farther back, out the rear windows, he could see nothing but a wall of yellow dust. He figured he had about a one-minute lead on the Murillos's soldiers.

It wasn't enough.

He needed at least four minutes if he was going to get the boys out with any margin of safety.

Ahead, the fine-dirt track plunged into a streambed lined with small stones. Either because it had been washed out or because this was Baja, the road *became* the streambed. Which was just fine with Bolan. The rocky bottom gave better traction on the turns, so he could go faster.

The speedometer's needle nosed past sixty.

He held it quivering there.

Because of the tightness of the curves and the obscuring, scraggy vegetation, every turn held the potential for a nasty surprise. Behind the wheel, the Executioner was hard-focused in his mind, but loose in his body. And way into his game. Given the terrain and his rate of speed, thinking was out of the question, all decisions made by instinct.

As the Suburban's rear end started to slide wide left, instinct told him to tromp the brakes.

Bolan powered out of the wild fishtail skid, crashing through and flattening a stand of parched, leafless, scrub trees that lined the bank. Ahead, the streambed cut an abrupt right. Rounding it, Bolan saw the road emerging from the channel twenty yards ahead.

He turned the wheel hard, putting the Suburban into a sideways, four-wheel drift, which ended when it bounded out of the streambed and up onto the road. Clear of the channel, with no curves ahead, Bolan mashed the accelerator flat. On either side of him, the cliffs fell away, as did the scrub trees. Accelerating, he continued to climb and the landscape broadened even farther, opening onto a sun-blasted plain. In the distance a series of low mountains stood between him and the extraction site.

Ahead the road was straight. It wasn't made of soft, poorly compacted, riverbed soil, but rather, hard-packed dirt over bedrock. A virtual superhighway. Bolan took full advantage, really pouring it on, taking the diesel engine to the max. He was doing almost a hundred up the slight grade when he checked his mirror. A couple of miles back, on the far side of his dust cloud, three sets of headlights trailed him.

He wasn't going to be able to gain the time he needed. He simply couldn't go fast enough to get the job done.

Over the crest of the first mountain and down the far side, the road began to wind again. Which put him into switchback mode again. Only now the terrain dropped precipitously off the sides of the road. Of course, there were no guardrails. No shoulders. A wrong move on his part, a misjudgment, would send the Suburban rolling down the mountainside. There were no trees to stop that kind of out-of-control descent; unchecked, the SUV would roll all the way to the bottom. If they survived the crash, they wouldn't survive the bullets of Murillos's thugs.

He had to slow down.

Six minutes passed, six minutes of back-to-back hairpin turns, then the range's highest mountain loomed before him. As mountains went, it wasn't much—no more than a thousand feet high. About two hundred yards from the summit, the road straightened and narrowed as its angle steepened.

Bolan downshifted and, with engine howling, attacked the steep grade. Rocks protruding from the roadway ahead of him were worn slick, covered with black streaks, layers of rubber left by madly spinning tires. The going was so rough the last twenty feet that he had to slow down or break an axle. Then, with a baritone growl, the Suburban lurched over the crest.

Reaching flat ground, he immediately skidded the vehicle to a stop. After jerking up the emergency brake, he reached for the muzzle of the M-89 sniper rifle.

"Don't move," he warned the boys as he bailed out of the SUV. "I'll be right back." He left the driver's door open, its warning bell chiming.

Bolan uncapped the ends of the Leupold scope as he

trotted back to the top of the hill. Locking his left arm into the rifle's sling, he knelt in the middle of the roadway.

Below him, over the crest of a lower peak, three vehicles with headlights on roared up the track in tight formation. He waited for them to close on his position. In the lead was a full-size, Chevy pickup. Two guys rode in the cab. Two more rode in the truck bed. Bolan held off until the pickup was well into the narrow, high-sided, channel road—until it had started to climb the grade to the summit—then he lined up the sight's center post on his target and curling his index finger around the trigger, smoothly took up the slack.

The heavy rifle punched him hard in the shoulder. He rode the recoil wave, automatically working the bolt and cycling the action, while, 150 yards downrange, from corner to corner, the driver's side of the Chevy's windshield turned opaque.

It wasn't bulletproof.

The smoking brass cartridge was still airborne as Bolan reacquired the sight picture. He fired again, putting the second slug a bit lower than the first. The windshield buckled and collapsed inward, but didn't completely fall out of its frame. Instantly, the Chevy lost speed and control. Its left side ground against the side of the channel, screeching, sparking on the half-buried rocks. Then it came to a stop. As it did so, the horn sounded.

And kept on sounding.

Something heavy—a deadweight—was leaning against it.

The two men riding in the pickup's bed hopped out and hid behind it.

Ejecting the spent cartridge, the Executioner dropped his aim and punched a hole in the middle of the truck's radiator. A jet of steam spurted out, followed by a gush of rusty water.

The Chevy's horn stopped blowing as somebody in the

front seat pulled the dead driver off the steering wheel. The maneuver also had the effect of shifting the driver's feet. Almost at once, the truck began to roll backward, down the hillside channel. The guys hiding behind the truck jumped out of the way, flattening themselves against the bank to keep from being crushed. Because he was tangled up with the driver's body, the passenger couldn't get his foot planted on the brakes. The Chevy rapidly picked up speed, then crashed into the Suburban stopped behind it.

The Executioner had his four minutes.

Maybe more, by the time the Murillo soldiers untangled the Chevy and got it out of their path.

Bolan climbed back into the Suburban, laying the M-89 across the front passenger's seat. "Everything's going to be okay," he said, looking over the seat. The older boy was holding his little brother's hand, both of them so terrified they were shaking.

There was nothing he could do about that. Nothing he could say to change the fact that the rough ride wasn't over yet.

"Just hang on, you two," he said, shifting the diesel into gear. "Hang on a little longer."

ROBERTO MURILLO saw stars as the side of his head smashed into the passenger's window. There was a sharp pain at the base of his neck. A pain that spiked as the tipped-up Suburban came crashing back down on all four wheels.

Into a raging sea of flame.

It only lasted a couple of seconds. Miraculously, they burst through the wall of fire and into the clear desert air. The SUV's hood and right fender were covered with blisters and scorch marks. The windshield wipers had melted onto the glass. The window beside his head was fire-blackened and cracked from the impact with his skull. He had to roll down the window to see out.

Looking back on that side, he saw nothing but devastation. A plume of roiling, oily black smoke two hundred feet wide rose skyward, and surrounding it, a lake of flame danced over what had been the end of the airstrip. The hangar was gone. Obliterated along with the fuel dump. Pieces of its metal skin were still raining to earth.

Murillo's driver cut the wheel sharply, following the taillights of the Chevy pickup in front, which was following the intruder's SUV.

Murillo glanced over the seat out the rear windows, to see if the other pickup truck was still there. It was. Smoke billowed from its open windows. As the last one through the fireball, it had taken the brunt. He could make out the men inside the cab beating themselves frantically, trying to put out the flames.

The mass of dust raised by the vehicles ahead of them obscured the gatehouse until they were practically on top of it. In a flash, Murillo saw that the gate was no longer there. It had been ripped off its hinges. And thirty feet away, one of his sentries lay pinned beneath the twisted metal, which lay jammed against the side of a tall saguaro. The man wasn't feeling the cluster of cactus spikes that had pierced his cheek and left eye. His head was twisted at an unnatural angle, chin turned over his right shoulder.

The Suburban roared on.

Murillo sank back into his seat, pleased that he had had the foresight to send the sniper. To arrange for a police welcoming committee at the foot of Bahia Concepción.

The driver slowed at the bottom of the grade, swerved around the bend, then headed west up the canyon.

With the window down and the back bumper of the Chevy only thirty yards ahead, it was serious, dust-eating time for everyone in the Murillo Suburban. Clouds of grit rolled in before Murillo got the window back up. It floured their faces, hands and clothes with malted milk-colored powder. Even with the windows up and the air vents closed, fine dust seeped through every seam and crack in the vehicle's chassis.

There was no way Murillo's driver could get around the Chevy pickup. The road was too narrow, and there were no turnouts. To pull off on either side of the two-rut track meant getting stuck in sand or having a tire blow out from cactus thorns.

As the SUV slalomed back and forth through the turns, Roberto Murillo gripped the handhold above the passenger's door. There was absolutely nothing to do but ride until the lead pickup caught up with the Suburban, or they drove it under the guns that would be waiting at Highway 1. Which gave Murillo time to evaluate what had happened and why.

"How many intruders died upstairs in the rancho?" he demanded of the men in the back seat.

The question was met by an uncomfortable silence.

"What was the size of the force that attacked us?" he persisted.

After another moment of silence, the soldier in the middle replied stiffly, "I only saw our own men dead, Patron. No one else."

The other two soldiers nodded.

"Couldn't you have missed their bodies under all the fallen debris?"

"We dug our way out of the collapsed hallway, Patron," the middle soldier said. "If there were dead enemies there, we would have had to crawl over their corpses."

"Who were you firing on up there, then?"

"The tall man who took the children. I can't speak for anyone else, but he was the only one I saw."

To Murillo's astonishment, the other soldiers confirmed that they, too, had only seen and shot at the one intruder.

"You expect me to believe that there was *no* attacking force? Look back there! Look!" He jabbed a finger toward the SUV's rear window. The smoke from the burning rancho and the destroyed fuel dump blotted out a quarter of the sky. "You're telling me that one man did all that? That thirty of you couldn't stop one man?"

Intimidated by the ferocity of his outburst, Murillo's men stared at their shoes.

"Idiots!" he snarled in disgust as he turned away.

Roberto Murillo knew he was in big trouble. Samosa had no patience with failure. He had lost control of the Don's offspring, as well as control over his patron's former mistress and her evidence. That one man had been permitted to inflict such damage to their cause made matters even worse. The Lord of the Seas had no patience with incompetence, either.

The chief cause of his problems was Yovana Ortiz. If she passed on to the Feds what she knew about the bribery network it would bring his entire operation crashing down. Samosa was understandably much less concerned by this prospect. And not just because he was thinking about his own flesh and blood. The international drug lord could go on without Mexico; Mexico was all the Murillo brothers had.

There was only one way to make things right.

Everyone in the other Suburban had to die.

Murillo's logic was as simple as it was implacable. As long as the boys were alive, they could be rescued. And they *would* be rescued, sooner or later. The goddamned U.S. Navy could do it that very night by intercepting the ship Samosa had sent to pick up his children when it motored south, out of the Sea of Cortez. If the boys were dead, they couldn't be rescued and the immediate threat to the Murillos was dispensed with. As long as the truth about their fate was kept from Ortiz, believing they were still alive she would keep her mouth shut, at least for a while.

Long enough for Ramon to take her out.

Of course, difficult explanations would have to be made to Samosa. Difficult and dangerous, but not impossible.

Roberto and his brother owned the local police, top to bottom, and since there was no qualified medical examiner for five hundred miles in either direction, the murders could be easily covered up. If, after it was captured, the Suburban crashed and burned with the bodies inside, all the blame would go to the kidnapper. While trying to escape, the tall American simply ran off the road.

End of story.

As they dropped over the backside of a mountain, Murillo got a glimpse of red taillights on top of the next summit.

"We're gaining on him," the driver said.

The man behind the wheel of the Chevy had to have seen the flash as well. He reacted by stomping on the gas, pulling away from the Suburban as he tried to close the gap.

"Faster!" Murillo said. "Stay with him!"

The winding turns gave way to a straight, slightly downhill stretch of road. At its bottom, the big grade to the peak began. Above them, at the top of the run, the dark-green Suburban disappeared over the summit.

Caught unaware, Murillo was thrown forward against his shoulder belt as his own vehicle hit the first, upraised boulder. The SUV twisted and wrenched over the obstacle. Ahead were many more. And thc road's angle steepened. The Suburban shimmied back and forth as its wheels fought for traction on the slick, uneven surface, fought to continue the climb.

Then the pickup on the grade in front of them suddenly slowed. Murillo's driver let out a curse and slammed on his brakes. The Suburban lurched to a stop, as did the pickup behind.

Murillo heard the sound of a horn. He cranked down his window and stuck his head out. As he did, the men riding in the bed of the Chevy bailed out. "What the hell is going on?" he shouted at them.

The brake lights of the truck winked off at the same instant the horn stopped sounding. Almost at once, the pickup started rolling backward, down the narrow channel.

Roberto Murillo pulled his head back in a second before the unavoidable impact.

HANGING ON to the handlebars of the ATV, Drigo Martinez jumped up and dropped his full weight on the kick-start pedal. The motor turned over, but failed to catch. As he pulled out the choke, he could hear the crackle of automatic weapon's fire from the garage and the roar of a diesel engine.

Grunting with the effort, he heaved himself up and dropped on the pedal again.

No dice.

The gunfire from the garage stopped. The engine grew rapidly softer, fading into the distance. From the sound, Martinez knew the intruder was getting away.

A few yards from where the sniper stood, the previous driver of the ATV lay in the dirt on his back. His head and chest were riddled with bullet holes and the blood that soaked his T-shirt was already turning black in the sun. The crotch of his shorts was stained where in death he had wet himself.

That's me, Martinez thought with a shudder. That's me if I fuck up.

He pushed the choke back in and hurled himself at the kick-start.

The ATV rumbled to life. Martinez revved it hard, then held the throttle wide open, making sure it kept running. As he secured the strap of the H&K sniper rifle across his back, he heard other trucks starting up. By the time he dropped the ATV in gear and shot away from the rancho, all four vehicles—one fleeing, three pursuing—were stretched in a line across the far end of the airfield.

Then the fuel dump blew.

Even though he was a half mile away, Martinez felt the shock wave and the blast of heat. Instinctively covering his face with his hand, he let the ATV roll to a stop. It looked as if a miniature nuke had gone off, what with the immense fireball and the mushroom cloud of churning black smoke.

From around the far side of the flames, the dark-green Suburban appeared. It had changed direction and was now headed for the main gate, which the sentries were in the process of closing. As he watched, all three of the chase vehicles had burst through the fireball and turned after their prey.

Martinez thought the dark-green Suburban had no chance.

Then its driver took out the gate and both sentries, and roared on down the road.

For better or worse, the ball was in Martinez's court.

He twisted the accelerator hard, popping an unintentional wheelie. When the front tire touched down, he wound the ATV through a quick succession of stomach-wrenching, max-throttle gear shifts over the relatively flat ground. He was doing close to seventy as he approached the midsection of the airstrip. To his left, the trio of Murillo trucks disappeared through the broken gateway in a cloud of dust.

Once he crossed tarmac, Martinez followed one of the patrol paths used by the sentries. The track rose and fell over the hummocks of the desert plain and cut across some fairly wide arroyos, which forced him to back off his speed a little, but the route ran straight at the bright line of fence four miles away. Which meant he could gain some ground on the Suburban, which had to traverse the winding canyon.

The fence marked the western perimeter of the rancho. Beyond it, the terrain got much less hospitable.

Martinez skidded to a stop beside the fence's steel gate. It only took him a moment to throw the bolt and shoot through the gap. A much fainter, less traveled path continued on the other side.

Winding out the engine in second gear, he flew over the next rise. And kept on flying, over the edge of a deep gully. As the earth dropped away beneath him, he rocked up on the ATV's footrests. He landed flat on all three wheels on the arroyo's stony channel. There was no way out the other side, just a sheer dirt wall topped with stunted scrub. He turned left and rampaged down the dry streambed, ducking the dust-covered, leafless tree limbs that threatened to sweep him from his seat.

When he found a gap in the bank and foliage, he blasted through it and raced uphill, swerving around the big boulder outcrops.

Martinez poured on the speed, his back wheels throwing up sandy soil as he cut his own path to the summit. When he popped over the crest of the hill, he hit the brakes. Below, he could see a line of beige cutting across the brown plain at the edge of the low mountains. The old San Bartolomeo road had been abandoned years ago because the runoff from the brief but intense seasonal rains always washed it out.

He roared down the steep slope, weaving around obstacles, jumping the small gullies. When he reached the abandoned road, he really opened up the speed. It was a dangerous thing to do because of the deep ruts and washouts. Martinez kept his eyes focused way ahead, and when he saw a problem looming, he steered off the road to get around it. Sometimes this meant a considerable cross-country detour.

He'd traveled five miles when the mountain range to his left began to dwindle and disappear back into the plain. In the distance ahead he could see the last high hill before Bahia Concepción. It was the eroded remnant of a small volcano. It overlooked the road the dark-green Suburban was running.

And his killzone.

When Martinez got to the hill, he zigzagged up. He

stopped the ATV just short of the summit and shut off the engine. When he dismounted, he felt the back of his shirt soaked through with sweat; his legs trembled from the wild ride. He could taste the dirt in his mouth, feel it against his teeth. He took off his dusty sunglasses and cleaned them on his shirttail. Then he looked east along the dirt road below.

Shielding his eyes from the glare off the land, he could make out a minitornado at the base of the nearest mountain. The dust cloud was a mile away and closing. Behind him was the brilliant turquoise disk of Bahia Concepción. The southernmost tip of the huge, placid bay stood between him and Highway 1. The San Bartolomeo road continued straight and flat past the bottom of Martinez's hill, skirting the waterline by a hundred yards.

He unslung his H&K G-3 SG/1 and, moving to the edge of the hilltop, found a solid shooting position behind a rocky outcrop. He uncapped the Zeiss telescope and surveyed the terrain downrange. On both sides of the road man-high stands of dried grasses and reeds were evidence of the water running underground there for at least part of the year. The reeds were sparse and would provide no real cover; the rest of the brush was knee-high. Martinez had a space of maybe an eighth of a mile in which to do his work.

He checked his weapon's 20-round magazine to make sure it was fully loaded. Then he shouldered the G-3 and peered through the scope. Martinez scanned the landscape downrange until he found a familiar object. The fifty-five-gallon metal drum lay on its side in the dirt. He put the crosshairs on it. Since Martinez knew how long the drum was by measuring its length using the scope, he could estimate the distance it was from him. He adjusted the Zeiss's bullet-drop compensator accordingly, turning the knob down one and a half clicks.

As he snugged into the shoulder sling, he began his preshoot routine. The ritual slowed and deepened his breathing. It allowed him to relax and to eliminate distractions. Start to finish, it took him no more than a minute to complete.

He dropped the G-3's safety, tightened the butt into his shoulder and looked through the scope.

Out of a cloud of roiling dust, the dark-green Suburban appeared. Martinez slid his finger inside the trigger guard and curled it around the familiar curve of metal. He could see the driver, a dark-haired man, behind the bullet-pocked, badly spiderwebbed windshield. The bulletproof glass was already structurally weakened.

All he had to do was hit the nail on the head.

Martinez swung his sights through the oncoming target. And when the crosshairs reached the middle of the Suburban's hood, he squeezed off his first shot.

19

Inside the moving van, it was hot and airless, and to Ramon Murillo it smelled like sweat, gun grease and tobacco smoke. Under their Kevlar riot helmets, with clear plastic visors tipped up, the faces of his eighteen hired guns were brown. Each wore full body armor, down to shin and forearm guards. They looked like Mexican samurai.

The colors and insignia on the battle gear indicated that it belonged to the Federal Judicial Police. It had all been looted from a barracks outside Tijuana, along with some heavy ordnance. Four of the men held U.S.-made M-60 machine guns; two others shouldered pairs of olive-green, LAW rocket tubes. The rest had Mexican-manufactured 7.62 mm Heckler & Koch assault rifles.

A set of schematics had been nailed up on the plywood-lined wall. The drawings would've been impossible to read had the trailer's dim overhead lighting not been boosted by a row of battery-powered lanterns. The individual blueprints showed the layout of the former president's estate, the two above-ground floors, the elevator and stairwell leading down and the below-ground level.

To Murillo, the shock troops looked raring to go. They were paying close attention to what the man with the pencil mustache was saying as he pointed at the schematics with a stick, indicating possible trouble spots and going over the job's primary objectives for the last time. Ramon Murillo found himself growing bored. He had already heard the speech twice.

The plan was to make a loud and spectacular entry into the ex-president's mansion through the front doors, forcing the above-ground Secret Service contingent to retreat to the lower level in order to protect their vital witness. It was unlikely that the Secret Service would stand and defend the turf. Rather, they would fight a delaying action to guarantee the safe retreat of Yovana Ortiz, before pulling back down the same passage themselves.

Murillo's mercenaries didn't have to worry about pursuing their quarry and her protectors through the maze of passages in the mansion's subterranean level. Their mission, though loud and violent, was nothing but a feint. The idea was to convince the gringo bodyguards that neither Ortiz nor they could survive if they tried to hold their ground. The idea was to convince them that their only hope was the back way out.

For the operation to work, everything had to happen very quickly. The man with the mustache underscored this for the troops. They were to press the attack with their overwhelming firepower. And once they'd gained entry to the building, a third of their number were to seal off access to the top floor and pin any opposition up there. Another six men would clear and defend a corridor to the stairway and elevator. The last six would use that corridor to carry in the high explosives.

The satchel charges sat along the base of the van's wall beside three opened ammunition crates.

The explosives were the whipped-cream icing on the feint cake. They would make the Secret Service think that their attackers were willing and able to bring down the entire mesa on top of them.

Such a thing would have been fine with Murillo, if there had been some way to guarantee Ortiz's death in the process. It was a simple, if unpleasant, fact of life that people survived collapsed tunnels. And under no circumstances could she be allowed to survive. To be sure that she was dead, Murillo had to witness her killing. As he had personally scripted that demise, he was looking forward to it.

The guy with the mustache wrapped up his speech. He looked at his watch. "We will go on my mark, in exactly twenty minutes. Four. Three. Two. One. Mark. Recheck your gear one more time before we deploy."

Murillo waved at the mustached man, then indicated with a jerk of his head that the soldier guarding the trailer's back doors should open one of them. A blast of bright, afternoon sunshine cut into the semigloom. Murillo slipped out the door and climbed down from the tailgate. His two bodyguards stepped up, and the three of them started up the street.

The mesa-top neighborhood, home to some of Tijuana's most elite citizens, was sparsely populated. The houses were few and huge, hidden by high solid walls. The ex-president's mansion was no exception. It had a twelve-foot concrete block wall.

Murillo and his men walked on the opposite side of the street. They passed the entrance to the mansion grounds. Massive steel gates stood between concrete posts. Two unmarked, three-quarter-ton vans with dark-tinted windows, obviously supplied by U.S. federal law enforcement, were parked nose to nose on the other side of the gate. They were positioned to block an attempt to crash open the gate with a larger vehicle. As Murillo stared, a scrambling pack of black-and-tan blurs shot between the vans and the inside of the gate—the rottweilers roamed free on the grounds. Which was the reason why the troopers had donned Kevlar shin and forearm guards.

The man known as Three Nails continued up the street to where his black Mercedes was parked. His driver hopped out and opened the right rear door for him.

After his bodyguards got in, they drove down the mostly

deserted boulevard. The center divider was landscaped with mature palm trees; water sprinklers oversoaked its lush green grass. As they descended to the bottom of the mesa, the road narrowed and its surface deteriorated. When they reached the bottom, the driver turned right.

As they rounded the curve, the bright tent canopies and flying pennants of the outdoor public market came into view. It backed against the foot of the mesa, in an empty dirt lot.

"Stop anywhere," Murillo said, putting on his sunglasses.

There were lots of cars and trucks parked half-on, half-off both sides of the street. The driver pulled onto the shoulder and stopped.

Murillo and the bodyguards got out of the Mercedes, then strolled toward the crowded market. Upbeat party music was playing. They turned down the first row of vendor stalls, where a wide variety of items were on display. Clothing, shoes and leather goods, housewares, audio cassettes, inexpensive jewelry and fresh produce were all set out on makeshift tables shaded from the sun.

They didn't stop at any of the stalls, but continued to the end of the row. At the back of the market, jammed right against the cliff, was a circular open area furnished with chairs and small metal tables. A pair of fast-food carts served hungry shoppers charcoal-grilled fish, meat tacos and cold drinks. Behind the carts, the gaily uniformed mariachi band had paused for a brief conference.

As Ramon Murillo moved between the tables, he saw Carlos's elderly mother. She was dressed in a white peasant blouse and gaudy, flower-print skirt. She had rouged her sallow, sickly cheeks and painted her lips bright red. She was selling bunches of cut flowers, roses and carnations, from five-gallon plastic buckets set in a small children's wagon. As he walked past her, Murillo smiled. It occurred to him that his own mother, the mother who had deserted him, would have been about the same age had she lived.

Murillo and his two companions took chairs at a table on the edge of the eating area. To his left, on the other side of the market, sat a dark-blue van with black-tinted windows and California license plates. Fed wheels. He figured Secret Service men would be stationed inside the getaway vehicle. To his right, across thirty yards of open ground in front of the bluff, was the footpath that Ortiz would have to take. It led from the concealed exit along the bottom of the cliff, across the back edge of the market.

Murillo checked his watch. He still had five minutes. He waved over the girl who was taking food orders. "Would you bring me a bottle of Negra Modelo?"

"Of course, and for you gentlemen?"

"They don't want anything," Murillo told her.

His bodyguards didn't drink on the job. Besides, they were busy. Behind their sunglasses, they were surveying the crowd, looking for anyone who might present a threat.

When the lone, dark beer arrived, Murillo picked out the wedge of lime that had been jammed into the opened top and squeezed it into the bottle. He drank a long swallow. The beer was very cold.

Murillo felt on top of the world. He got a kick out of knowing what was about to happen. To be sitting there, surrounded by people who were laughing and enjoying themselves, and knowing that in a few minutes the scene was going to be major ugly, the crowd screaming and running in all directions.

All because of him.

As the mariachi band started playing, the seated people began to clap their hands and whistle. Trumpets blared.

Murillo knew what the killing of an important witness right under the nose of the U.S. government was going to do for his and his brother's reputations. After this day, throughout Mexico, it would be said there was no escaping the wrath of the Murillo brothers. No one could protect you from them if they wanted you dead. Not even the FBI. And Ortiz's grisly murder would serve as an example to others in the operation to keep their mouths shut. Pleased with himself, he leaned back in his chair and took another swallow of the cold beer.

Three Nails had a front-row seat for his very own show.

SOME THREE HUNDRED yards away, in a concrete room deep under the mesa, Hal Brognola sat at a table across from the Ortiz woman. He wore his poker face while they waited for Bolan to report back. He made a conscious effort to keep from looking up at the clock on the wall because every time he looked up, Yovana Ortiz did so, too. When their eyes happened to meet over the table, he didn't blink. He looked at her in a way that gave up nothing. Certainly not a hint of his own, considerable unease. It was another acting job on his part.

Brognola had been in the business of covert ops too long to expect that things in Loreto were going to go down without a hitch. If there was a way for shit to hit the fan, it would.

Good guys could die.

Ortiz's kids could die.

The mission was important enough to take those risks, otherwise, it would never have been authorized. Men like Mack Bolan and the team of former Secret Service agents weren't replaceable. The payoff was going to be the unraveling of the Samosa cartel's Mexican arm.

The downside was the possibility of complete failure— that Bolan wouldn't succeed in returning the kids alive to their mother. Brognola wasn't the kind of guy to go into battle without a backup plan.

No matter what happened in Loreto, he needed to get the Ortiz woman across the U.S. border where she could be more easily protected and where she could continue to be isolated from her family and friends. Removing her from Mexico was critical to getting his hands on her evidence. It didn't take a genius to figure out that Ortiz had stashed the material in the States in some secure, secret location. Perhaps in the hands of an attorney. Perhaps in a safety-deposit box. Perhaps buried under a rose bush. Bottom line, without her assistance, he was never going to find it.

He had orchestrated the same, hostile discovery process many times during his career at the Department of Justice. Usually with mobsters or their relatives. In this case it meant maintaining physical control of Yovana Ortiz while she mourned the loss, temporary or permanent, of her two children. Though she wasn't aware of it, yet, she would remain essentially his prisoner until she surrendered her video tapes. And in short order, Brognola would be doing the whole hostage number on her, in the nicest way possible. "Nice" meant isolate, intimidate, undermine. Everything short of physical torture. From past experience, he knew it could take weeks or even months to break her down and make her give up what she had.

Even though he despised the woman's crimes and the dirty money that had financed her life-style, Brognola wasn't some heartless, crusading avenger. He could relate to and had compassion for the loss and the pain she had already suffered in her attempt to break free of the Samosa cartel. He knew that in no small degree he was responsible for how things had gone down to this point, and if harm came to her kids, that would be partially his fault, too. He had definitely pushed the envelope with the Murillo brothers. Christ, he had unleashed the Executioner on them.

What gave the big Fed a sick, tight feeling in the pit of his stomach was the knowledge that the deaths of her children might be the best thing in the world for his case. If that tragedy happened, it would be his job to frame Samosa for the crime, to make Ortiz believe that he had ordered it. In order to accomplish that, he might have to manufacture evidence. He would probably have to intimidate other informants into lying. The whole bag of prosecutorial dirty tricks.

If Brognola could convince her that Samosa was behind the murders of her children, he was certain that she wouldn't protect him any longer. And if she wouldn't protect him, the drug kingpin became vulnerable. As important as it was to bring down the corrupt Mexican bureaucrats behind the cartel's drug pipeline, the ultimate goal was to bring down the Lord of the Seas himself. That goal had been determined to be in the national security interest of the United States, and to achieve it Brognola would use his broad, extralegal powers to do whatever was necessary.

He didn't make the rules. And he didn't get paid to debate them.

His job was to keep his eyes on the prize.

And the prize was the head of Jorge Luis Samosa.

20

Even though the dirt road before them had finally straightened out, Juanito's stomach was still feeling queasy, his head still spinning. The speed combined with the mountain curves had very nearly made him throw up. He tried to keep his eyes looking forward, out the bullet-pocked windshield at the horizon line. Though he didn't know exactly where they were, he had a rough idea how far away Tijuana was from Loreto. Somewhere close to five hundred miles. He knew it was too far for them to get there by road with men chasing after them. He wanted to ask Striker what they were going to do, how they were going to get away, but the tall man was driving so fast Juanito was afraid that the question might distract him for a second and make him crash the car.

On the other side of the bench seat, Pedro had slumped way down, chin on chest, eyes downcast. His skin was a funny color, pale and a little bit green. He was carsick, too.

"Look out the front window," Juanito told him. "It'll make you feel better."

No sooner than he gotten the words out than something slammed into the windshield with a solid *whack!*

It was a sound he remembered from the rancho's front gate.

A sound he would never forget.

Somebody was shooting at them.

As the realization sunk in, another crunching *whack* hit

the windshield. Only this time, a bright spot of light appeared in the center of the spiderweb of glass. And instantly, the wind through the new hole made a shrill, whistling sound.

Striker reacted to the sudden attack, jerking the steering wheel left, then right. The Suburban slewed off the road on one side, then off the road on the other. The violent sidelong lurches slammed the boys against the insides of the car doors and into the webbing of their seat-belt harnesses.

When the bouncing lessened, Juanito caught a silver glint in the right corner of the driver's headrest. The mushroomed nose of the bullet peeked out of the leather upholstery at him.

Then a hail of slugs tore into the SUV.

The impacts were so evenly spaced, they seemed almost rhythmic. Under the torrent, the right side mirror shattered and the front passenger's window caved inward. The hood over the engine compartment rattled as it was slashed by heavy-caliber bullets. Juanito could see bright marks around the holes where the paint had been blown off.

Striker didn't stop or slow down. There was no place to hide on the long, straight road. The Suburban's engine howled mightily as he accelerated even faster.

Bullets continued to rain down. The dashboard came apart, shattering the vent, heater and air-conditioning controls and CD player, sending plastic shrapnel flying through the SUV's cab.

Then there was a loud boom right below Juanito's seat. The car's rear end dropped on that side, and it started to fishtail wildly. A back tire had been shot out.

As Striker fought for control, the engine made a horrible metal-shearing clunk. Which was followed by a series of clunks. It sounded as though it was tearing itself apart.

The view out the windshield was suddenly cut off as the hood latch released and the hood popped. Caught by the wind, it lifted straight up in the air.

Unable to see the road, Striker crashed on the brakes. The nose of the heavy vehicle dipped, and Juanito was hurled forward against his safety belt, then back into the seat so hard that it made him see stars for a second.

He looked over at his brother. The expression on Pedro's face said he wanted his mama. Juanito did, too. He wanted to tell her about all the bad, scary things he'd seen, to get them out of his head and out of his heart. He wanted to be held by her, to be comforted by her, to sit on her lap with his head against her chest and have her touch his hair while she told him that everything was going to be okay.

Everything.

"Unbuckle your seat belts," Striker told them. "When I stop, I want you both to get out on my side. On *my* side. Get out and get on the ground. Stay next to the car. Don't move until I tell you."

Juanito had the feeling that the tall man was in charge, no matter what happened. He didn't seem scared. He didn't seem angry or upset. He seemed to know exactly what to do and when to do it.

It wasn't like he was having fun. It wasn't a game to him. He was deadly serious about what he was doing. He displayed a confidence that Juanito had only seen in one other person: his father. Even though the world was falling apart all around him, he was absolutely in control. The boy couldn't really comprehend that kind of self-containment on an intellectual level. But he understood it on an emotional level.

It was like he and his brother were in this man's house.

And inside Striker's house, nothing could touch them.

The Suburban skidded to a halt; its idling engine continued to make a terrible, grinding sound.

"Out! Out, now!" the tall man said.

LIKE A SURGEON, Drigo Martinez sliced the Suburban apart. As he swung the G-3 ahead of the moving target, he fired a steady stream of bullets. Because the SUV was bouncing up and down over the uneven road and swerving, it was difficult to put the shots exactly where he wanted them. Dust puffed up from the engine hood. Icelike sprays of shattered glass exploded from the windshield and tumbled, twinkling back over the roof.

Somewhere in the back of his mind, Martinez was counting the shots as the delayed blow-back action spit out brass hulls. He had already put eight rounds into the vehicle, when he managed to hit a tire. It was pure luck, of course. The dark-green Suburban nearly went out of control, but somehow the driver managed to keep it from flying off the road. The next few shots penetrated the middle of the hood, but even so, there was no guarantee that he had hit anything inside.

Then the hood popped up.

He knew he had them. He knew they would have to stop.

The Suburban slewed as the driver stomped his brakes. Again Martinez thought the SUV was going to go out of control in the soft dirt. Instead, the vehicle spun sideways into the reeds by the side of the road and came to a stop there in a cloud of dust.

Now I got you, Martinez thought, as he dumped the nearly empty magazine and quickly replaced it.

He had stationary targets to shoot at.

As Martinez settled in behind his rifle, he was already counting his half million bucks.

Through the Zeiss scope he could see the doors on the driver's side pop open and the people inside jump out. Although the top and chassis of the car gave them cover from his down-angled fire, the three targets had nowhere to go. He got a glimpse of the driver pulling a long gun from the front seat. In order to use it he was going to have to show himself.

Martinez fine-tuned the scope's bullet-drop compensator, using the broadside of the Suburban as a new mark.

When the man's head peeked up above the SUV's roof, he fired.

The slug's impact left a silver spot on the dark-green paint job. The way the man's head disappeared, Martinez doubted that he'd managed to skip the slug into the guy.

It didn't matter. He had a great shooting angle on the Suburban. The driver couldn't fire at him from underneath it and stay hidden. He had to shoot over the top of the roof or the hood. Or around the front or rear of the vehicle. Anyway he tried to do it, Martinez had him cold.

The sniper lowered his sights and fired once. The quick shot dropped the right front tire on its rim. It was more insurance that the vehicle wouldn't get far fast.

A head appeared around the front bumper. A head and the barrel of a rifle.

Martinez put the crosshairs on the head and squeezed the trigger.

The H&K rocked back into his shoulder. A fraction of an instant later, his shoulder was slammed again, this time higher, right on the joint. Pain exploded up his neck and down his back. The jolting impact drove him out from behind his cover, spun and dropped him flat on his butt on the ground.

Though red-hot agony shot through his shoulder, his arm was dead down to the fingertips, which dangled in the dirt. The scoped G-3 lay across his lap, but he couldn't reach for it.

When he looked at his shoulder, he realized that he'd been shot.

The top of his T-shirt sleeve had been sliced open. It looked as if a hand grenade had gone off under his skin. The 7.62 mm NATO round had blown his shoulder joint apart. He could see the angry red socket. The ball part of his shoulder, the connecting ligaments and deltoid muscle were in a million fragments, sprayed like sticky confetti over the rocks behind him.

Martinez had to move.

He was sitting out in the open, but he couldn't make his body work.

His legs wouldn't operate. His left arm, which hadn't been hit, had no strength. He couldn't even use it to make himself fall over on his side. The shock had paralyzed him. His mind, however, was running on all cylinders.

"Oh, God!" Martinez moaned.

He knew exactly what was coming.

He closed his eyes a second before the follow-up shot hit him square in the head.

BOLAN WORKED THE M-89's action, ejecting the spent cartridge and locking down the bolt on a live round. Braced against the Suburban's bumper, he reacquired the sight picture on the hilltop. The sniper now sat cross-legged in the open, three hundred yards away, outlined against the blue sky. He'd hit the man with a snap shot, aiming at the sun flash off the scope's lens. From his sixty-degree, upward angle of view, Bolan couldn't tell how much damage his first bullet had done, whether the guy was still alive or not. There wasn't time to wait and see. The sniper's position on the hill overlooked the road for a mile in either direction. Before they could move on, it had to be vacated.

The Executioner put the Leupold's crosshairs on the sniper's breastbone, tightened the trigger to the break point, then smoothly squeezed until the cap snapped. The sniper rifle jarred his shoulder. He rode the recoil wave, recentering his scope on the target. He had aimed the 168-grain boat-tail slug a little more than a foot low to compensate for the steep angle. On the edge of the hilltop, the seated sniper's head, from the eye sockets up, came apart. For an instant, a red puff of brain jelly hung backlighted by the afternoon sun. Then the body slumped onto its side.

Bolan straightened and, as he did so, glanced at the boys

who were crouching as low as possible beside the SUV. "Are either of you hurt?" he asked. "Are you both okay?"

Juanito and Pedro nodded.

"Great, then get back in the car," Bolan told them.

He stepped around to the front of the vehicle. Things looked pretty shot up under the hood. There were several bullet holes in the air cleaner and the valve covers. Below the bumper, antifreeze puddled on the ground, a stream of bright green sizzling into the sand.

It was a good thing they didn't have much farther to go, he thought as he slammed down the hood. It didn't close all the way, something had gotten twisted or broken, but it was close enough. When Bolan moved for the driver's door, he looked east. In the distance, over a rise in the road, he saw two vehicles coming at them.

He'd lost two precious minutes.

There was no way to get them back.

When he stepped on the accelerator, the Suburban started moving, but just barely. The noise from under the hood sounded like a jackhammer. With the damaged engine and its two flat tires on the right side, the SUV wouldn't go faster than thirty-five miles an hour.

As Bolan rounded the base of the volcanic hill, he got his first glimpse of the long bay. A short distance off the road, down near the waterline, an abandoned refrigeration trailer sat on cinder blocks. It was where the fishermen kept their catches cold until a truck came to pick it up.

As he turned off the road, thick, black smoke started pouring out from under the hood and up through the bullet holes that pocked it. The smoke rushed through the breaks in the windshield and began to fill the passenger compartment.

"We're going to have to get out and run real soon," he said over his shoulder, raising his voice to be heard over the pounding of metal on metal. "Can you run?"

No answer.

He looked up in the rearview mirror. "Can you run?" he shouted.

Juanito said, "We can run real fast."

The Suburban heaved a mighty forward jerk, then its motor died.

"Out!" Bolan said, throwing open his door.

The boys didn't have to be told twice.

As they bailed from the back seat, Bolan heard the familiar droning sound of an aircraft engine. He turned, looking past the end of the bay toward the western hills, and saw Grimaldi's Cessna skimming over their rounded summits. The plane dipped down the front of a slope and crossed Highway 1, flying right at them.

In order to reach the flat section of road where Grimaldi could safely land, the Executioner and the children had to run a quarter mile along the beach. There just wasn't enough time.

Over the Suburban's roof Bolan saw the two rancho vehicles closing on them. Flames had started to lick through the holes in the hood. He had to find some hard cover, and quickly. "That way!" he said, pointing toward the refrigeration unit. "Head for the trailer. Don't stop for anything. I'll be right behind you."

He was pleased to see that the boys could indeed run. He brought up the rear, dashing around the gaps in the waist-high brush, trying to keep his body between the enemy and the children.

Behind him on the road, the two vehicles screeched to a stop beside the Suburban, and someone started shouting. Bolan figured that automatic weapons fire would shortly follow.

He was right.

21

With lights and sirens flashing, Officer Chuey Mandelo barreled up the two-lane Highway 1 from Loreto. The cars and trucks ahead of him had no shoulder to pull off on, even if they had wanted to. Where the highway ended, the desert sand began. So the other vehicles had to slow even more, allowing the pair of police cars to pass, when they dared.

Officer Mandelo dared.

This was, after all, for early retirement.

And he was running late.

He swerved back and forth between his lane and the oncoming traffic, cutting around the slow cars. The second police cruiser rode right on his back bumper. To not ride his tail would have been suicide. On the wrong side of the road, doing better than ninety, Mandelo watched as the towering front grille of a semitractor screamed down on him. He sliced over into the right lane at almost the last moment. The second cop car, driven by Officer Aguiar, wouldn't have made the cut, if the truck driver hadn't swung out off the pavement.

Mandelo's partner and passenger, Hidalgo Diamante said, "Aye-aye-aye! Aye-aye-aye!" Diamante was seriously overweight. He couldn't button the front of his uniform anymore, not by a good six inches. Diamante kept checking the lock on his seat belt as the cruiser's under-inflated tires squealed around the tight, looping turns. And he was sweating profusely.

It was hot out, even for Baja in the summer.

Almost at the same instant the bay appeared ahead on the right, Mandelo hit the brakes, anticipating the turnoff for the San Bartolomeo road. The side road was unmarked, a hard right down onto the desert. Mandelo bounced the cruiser down the dirt road a hundred feet or so, then swung a wide arc and pulled across it. The second car did the same. Together, they completely blocked access to the highway.

As Officer Mandelo got out, he took his peaked, brown, uniform hat from the dash and twisted it firmly on his head. Then he dug a pair of cheap binoculars out from under his seat.

"Hey, Chuey, look!" Diamante said as he straightened, pointing down the incline toward the bay.

Mandelo focused the binoculars. A short distance up from the shoreline, he saw a car on fire. It was the same dark-green Suburban they were supposed to keep from getting on the highway. A pickup truck and another SUV had stopped behind it, and armed men, whom he recognized as soldiers from the Murillo rancho, were piling out the doors. Roberto Murillo, himself, was leading them. Mandelo caught a glimpse of a lone figure running away from them, through the brush, toward the water. It was the assassin, he had no doubt. The odds against the wanted man looked to be about ten to one.

Mandelo felt a good deal let down when he realized this. His thunder was about to be stolen. If he had no hand in the apprehension of the killer, it would negatively impact his plans for retirement.

Automatic gunfire crackled from below.

"Amigos, get out the rifles!" he shouted at his fellow officers.

Diamante shuffled around to the trunk of the cruiser. He wore his pants very low, under the overhang of his great belly, and because of this, the cuffs dragged on the ground, which caused them to become frayed to a fringe over his heels. He popped the trunk and took out a Mexican-manufactured Heckler & Koch assault rifle. He was about to pass it over to Mandelo when a noise from above made him hesitate.

Out of the glare of the sun, a single-engine plane zoomed low over the crest of the hills on the other side of the highway, then swooped down at them at high speed.

Instinctively, Diamante dropped hard onto one knee as the plane passed twenty feet over their heads. It came so close that its prop wash ripped off Mandelo's hat.

Mandelo squinted against the stinging spray of grit it raised. He was forced to chase after his officer's hat, which started rolling away from him down the road. As he did so, spewing more curses, the plane's pilot pulled out of the shallow dive, banked sharply, then turned north up the bay.

As his Suburban crested the top of the last mountain, Roberto Murillo looked down on the long stretch of straight road ahead. He had yelled himself hoarse bullying and threatening his driver into going faster around the dangerous mountain curves to make up the ground they had lost on their quarry. The crash with the Chevy pickup on the summit had broken both of the Suburban's headlights and caved in the grille. Luckily, all the damage had been cosmetic: the radiator had escaped unharmed. The problem was the bullet-riddled truck completely sealed off the roadway. Murillo had had his men hook a tow rope to the Chevy's rear bumper and then used the Suburban to drag it backward down the narrow, rock-lined channel to a point where the sides of the road leveled out. With one of the soldiers steering the pickup, Murillo's driver had bumped it onto the sandy shoulder, out of the way.

With the confusion after the crash, the whole road-clearing operation had eaten up close to five minutes. By the end of which time Murillo was close to having a stroke.

Sure, he had sent a sniper ahead to cover the dirt road.

Sure, he had ordered some of the local police on his payroll to block off the access to the highway.

But there was far too much at stake here for him to rely completely on hired help. To make sure the job was done right, he needed to get his hands bloody.

Murillo had figured that his sniper would set up a hide on the barren hilltop looming on the right. From its summit, he could control the terrain in both directions. So, Murillo wasn't surprised to see the dark-green Suburban stopped in the distance. Even from a half mile away, he could see its hood up.

So could the other passengers. "Drigo nailed the bastard!" Chip cried from the backseat.

But he had spoken too soon.

As Murillo watched, the SUV's hood dropped down, a figure jumped in, and the vehicle started up the road, moving very slowly.

"Man, they're just crawling away!" Ryan exclaimed. "Drigo must've really fucked them up."

Murillo wondered why the sniper had stopped firing. It was an idle thought. At this point, it didn't matter what Martínez did or didn't do. If the cops were in position at the entrance to the highway, there was no place for the American to run. He could only turn up the shoreline road on the peninsula side of the bay. A gravel road that dead-ended after twenty-one miles at Punta Concepción.

Outnumbered and outgunned, the tall gringo would soon be run to ground and summarily slaughtered, along with his two young passengers.

As they rapidly gained on the limping vehicle, it turned off the main road and lumbered down toward the water. Murillo could smell burning rubber and scorched paint. The dark-green Suburban was on fire. Its brake lights flashed on.

"He's stopping!" Chip said. "We've got him!"

Before they could close the gap, the doors of the dark-green SUV popped open. The tall man and the two boys spilled out and started running through the bush.

Murillo's driver slammed on his brakes. Behind him, the driver of the pickup did likewise, narrowly avoiding a collision. Before the two vehicles came to complete stops, their occupants were already jumping out. Stepping up like a raggedy firing squad, Chip, Ryan, Edwards, Carlson, and the five surviving Murillo drug soldiers raised their automatic weapons and took aim.

"Kill them!" Murillo croaked, hoarsely. "Kill them all!"

The assault rifles on both sides of Murillo snarled. Strings of slugs combed the belt-high brush, rustling through the branches like a breeze straight from Hell.

22

As Bolan had expected, automatic weapon's fire crackled at his back. Strings of slugs clawed the air on either side of him. The rain of gunshots churned the sand between him and the children. There were too many guns and way too many bullets for them to outrun. The Executioner stopped short. Turning, he dropped to a knee. And as he did so, he swung the M-89 halfway up to his shoulder.

Looking over the scope instead of through it, in the space of a heart beat, Bolan measured his opposition. There were ten guys lined up in front of the stopped vehicles, their faces half hidden by a cloud of gunsmoke. Through the smoke ten muzzles winked star bursts at him. He didn't even think about using the Leupold; he was too close to his targets, and acquiring them in the view field would have taken time. Time that he didn't have.

It didn't matter which gunmen he shot. But he needed to drop a couple quickly to get his point across—that if the Murillo soldiers wanted to keep sucking air, they'd better start looking for hard cover.

The heavy rifle bucked against his grip.

His target was the white-bearded expatriate firing at him from behind the passenger's door of the Suburban. Bolan's NATO round dimpled the outside of the door, hitting Chip low in the stomach. The impact bounced Chip off the door frame and he lost hold of his autorifle. When he hit the ground, he rolled up into a tight ball.

By the time he started screaming blue blazes, Bolan had cycled the M-89's action and adjusted his aim. He fired again.

In the middle of the pack, one of the Mexicans jerked violently backward, arms flying outward, weapon cartwheeling away. For an instant, his legs pumped. It looked as if he was backpedaling, trying to regain his balance and recover from the stunning blow to his chest, but his knees wouldn't hold his weight.

As he crashed to the earth, the Executioner was already up and moving. Without the M-89. He left the sniper rifle on the sand. It was too heavy and too slow for the job at hand. As he ran to catch up with the boys, he unclipped the MAC-10 from the lanyard around his neck.

Behind him, the guns had gone suddenly silent. The only sounds were the screams of the two mortally wounded men.

Bolan had bought himself a window of opportunity, but it was narrow. And rapidly closing. Ahead of him in the scrub, Juanito and Pedro scampered over the white mounds of clam shells and veered toward the abandoned refrigerator trailer.

Before Bolan could reach the shell piles, the opposition recovered. Bullets smashed into the shells in front of him. He launched himself, diving over the top of the heap with slugs whining over his head. He landed on his stomach with a bone-jarring thump, bounced, then whirled to face the shooters.

He popped up over the top of the mound with the Ingram chattering in his fist. He sprayed bullets along the sides of the vehicles. A quick burst intended to make them think twice before they came after him.

As he ducked he saw three of the gunmen slipping away down the road toward the highway. They were trying to outflank him. If they managed to do that, they could get to the trailer and the children.

Bolan scrambled up and sprinted for the shore. Slugs

skipped past him and zipped across the surface of the bay. The autofire stopped after he'd crashed through the brush along the high-tide berm and vaulted to the shoreline. The berm hid him from the view of the shooters. In order to get him back in their sights, they would have to follow him.

The sand near the waterline was hard-packed, which allowed him to run faster. He'd covered about half the distance to the trailer when, from behind, he heard the sounds of engines starting up. And he knew that Roberto Murillo and his soldiers weren't just going to follow him—they were going to bring their rolling cover.

The Executioner made a split-second decision. Instead of continuing along the shore to the trailer, he clambered back over the berm and cut across the desert. His line of travel would have intersected the road, eventually. But he didn't get that far. Ahead, he saw the three men slipping through the brush, stealthily working their way down to the beach.

Though they didn't know it yet, they were the ones who'd been outflanked.

Bolan kept running, adjusting his angle of attack. He charged right at the nearest drug soldier. The guy looked up as he burst out of the bushes, sprinting the last four yards.

By then it was too late.

Running full-tilt, Bolan fired the MAC-10 single-handed with his arm outstretched. The SMG clattered five times. Two of the bullets went wide, missing the man's shoulders by inches. The other three stitched across throat and collarbone.

Not an instant killshot, but the guy went down hard.

Because the second gunman was thirty feet from Bolan's end of the skirmish line, he had a bit more warning than the first guy. He managed to get his assault rifle up to his shoulder before the Executioner was on top of him. He never got off a shot. Bolan fired from six feet away, and a cluster of slugs plowed into the middle of the man's chest.

Dust puffed from his shirtfront as he staggered sideways and dropped. He was dead before he hit the ground.

The third guy had the most warning of all. And seeing what was charging down on him, seeing what had been done to his compadres, he opted out of the whole deal. Changing direction, he raced for the beach and the cover of the high-tide berm.

Bolan stood to his full height and shifted the submachine gun to his left hand while he drew his Beretta 93-R from shoulder leather. The guy's bobbing head and shoulders were visible as he beat it through the brush. Bolan swung the pistol's sights through the target and maintaining the moving lead, squeezed the trigger. The 93-R made a sharp crack. A ricochet whined off the sand as the action cycled. He tracked the running man and squeezed. The pistol cracked again.

The second slug made a slapping sound, lead on flesh, a sound that Bolan knew well. The guy's head and shoulders disappeared behind the bushes. He hit the ground with an audible thump.

Behind him, engines roared. The pickup truck and the Suburban had turned off the road and were lumbering across the scrubland, angling in on the trailer.

The Executioner ran for the beach, and when he had harder ground underfoot, he really poured on the speed. The boys were waiting for him on the water side of the low trailer, huddled against the concrete blocks of its foundation. It was a scabby-looking thing. Rust showed under its peeling paint and it smelled of rotten fish.

"We were scared you were shot," Juanito said.

"I'm fine," he said. The sweat was pouring off him now that he had stopped running. He had to wipe his hands on his pants.

"We don't want to die, Striker," Juanito told him. "We want to see our mama again."

"You're not going to die," Bolan assured him. "And you'll see your mama, soon."

"Promise?"

"Yeah, I promise." He was concerned about Juanito's younger brother, who looked as if he might be slipping into shock. "It's okay, Pedro," Bolan said, patting the child on the shoulder. "We're all going to get out of this."

At the sound of car horns blaring, the little boy jerked as if struck.

The horns were a signal.

An open-fire signal.

Autofire stuttered. A barrage of slugs hammered the far side of the trailer. The ancient steel was useless. Bullets flew through the corroded metal as if it were tissue paper.

"Stay low!" Bolan said, pushing the boys flat to the ground below the double row of concrete blocks.

The trailer's walls shuddered above them. Plate-size chunks of steel blasted free while pieces of metal rained on their heads. The bullets skipped over the water behind them.

Backed against the bay, sandwiched on either side by gunmen, they had nowhere to run. From the blind ferocity of the attack, Murillo's soldiers seemed hell-bent on killing the children as well as him. Had the circumstances been different, in order to protect their lives, he might have considered throwing down his guns. But that option wasn't available.

Surrender wouldn't save them.

JACK GRIMALDI swung the Cessna over the bay in a wide turn. Though not nervous by nature, his pulse rate was up around two hundred beats a minute. Even over the roar of his engine, he could make out the crackle of automatic-weapon fire. His first pass over the beach had told him that Bolan was way outgunned, that he no longer had wheels, and that he was cut off from the makeshift runway Grimaldi intended to use. And the cop cars parked off the highway weren't there to protect and serve the innocent. He knew that. If they had been, they would have already intervened.

As Grimaldi came around to the south, he dropped the plane's nose for a better look.

Things had gotten worse.

Much worse.

Bolan and the kids crouched behind a battered trailer, pinned down by bracketing gunfire coming from behind a pickup and an SUV.

Grimaldi knew what he had to do. He throttled up and banked for the highway, and when he reached it, he banked again, coming around on the same tack he had the first time, over the shoreline at the south end of the bay. When he had himself lined up, he opened the sliding window in his door. Steering with his left hand, he reached across to the copilot's seat, where a small, olive drab-painted crate was strapped down with the seat harness. He flipped off the lid and dug through the excelsior for a pair of fragmentation grenades, which he dumped in his lap.

Switching hands on the control yoke, he picked up both frags in his left hand. He used his teeth to pull the safety pins, while holding down the grip safeties.

The pickup truck was a hundred yards ahead and a hundred feet below him. He waggled the Cessna's wings, shaving off sixty feet of altitude. As he swooped, he let both of the grip safeties off. The gunmen behind the pickup and the Suburban turned to look up at him. Then they raised their weapons. The two vehicles were no more than seventy-five feet apart. Given his airspeed, they might as well have been parked side by side.

Timing his drop, Grimaldi chucked the grenades out the window. He pounded the throttle down, and banking hard, veered away from the beach and out over the bay.

Four seconds passed. Then, from behind him came the thunderclaps, an instant apart.

FROM THE COVER of the Suburban, Roberto Murillo punched careful, single shots along the base of the trailer, hoping to clip the top of a head on the other side. Out of the corner of his eye, he caught the flash of the sun off the Cessna's windshield. He paused, lowering the sights of his M-16. The plane had turned toward them and was losing altitude as it paralleled the shoreline. The sight made the other men shooting from behind the vehicles pause and look up.

The Cessna swooped down, accelerating at them.

As Murillo turned and reshouldered his weapon, something dropped from the pilot's window. Something small and black, the size of a baseball. Before the object landed beside the pickup, before he could fire, the plane had passed overhead, whipping him with a stinging gust of wind.

Because he had to shut his eyes or be blinded, Murillo didn't see the second grenade, which hit the ground ten feet behind him.

The first explosion rocked the pickup truck, blasting off its doors, sending men flying. Murillo saw the flash, then, a half second later, was slammed from the rear. His forehead crashed into the Suburban's roof and he blacked out for an instant.

When he came to, he was kneeling on the sand, his ears ringing, the back of his head numb. Turning, he saw the men sprawled on the ground behind him. Their bodies had protected him from the blast and had absorbed most of the shrapnel. Edwards and Ryan lay facedown in the sand, their torsos oozing blood from a hundred slashes. Fat Carlson sat clutching his autorifle, his face blackened with soot. He opened and closed his mouth, but no sound came out. Blood poured down the front of his T-shirt from a gaping red gash across his throat, a gash that ran from ear to ear.

The other survivor was Mexican. He lay flat on his back, arms and legs outstretched, and moaned pitifully. He appeared to be paralyzed from the chest down.

When Murillo tried to stand, pain speared him and he realized that he'd been hit in the back of the right knee. He pulled himself up beside the Suburban. Over the roof, he glimpsed the tall gringo and the two boys sprinting along the shoreline toward the highway.

The plane circled out over the water. As it headed back for the beach, its speed dropped.

It was going to try to land on the road! Murillo thought. It was going to land and pick up the children!

Grabbing his weapon, he tried to follow them. He could only hop, because of his injured leg.

Murillo got about fifty feet before the pain made him stumble. He fell to the sand, breaking his fall with the M-16. From ground level, he could no longer see the three running figures, but parked across the road about a quarter mile away were the two police cars he'd ordered.

"Shoot! Do something!" he cried. "Do something, damn you!"

OFFICER MANDELO and his colleagues watched in astonishment as the small plane made its bombing run against the Murillo soldiers. They were similarly stunned as the Cessna U-turned and descended, apparently to attempt a landing on the dirt road.

"He will crash and burn," Diamante predicted.

The plane's engine throttled back to idle. The aircraft came in smoothly. The touchdown of its wheels was as light and delicate as a feather.

"He's good," Mandelo said. "He's really good."

The Cessna bounced over the rutted road. It slowed but kept on rolling. The pilot expertly turned the plane around, then stopped it. Powering the engine up to takeoff rpms, he held the aircraft stopped with the foot brakes.

Mandelo raised his binoculars. He could see a man and two boys running up from the beach, running for the plane. Beside him, Diamante and Aguiar braced their assault rifles on the front fenders of the cruisers and took aim at the aircraft. He turned the binoculars on the downed Murillo forces. He scanned the scrub, but couldn't see anyone moving. It looked as if everyone was dead.

It occurred to Mandelo that if Roberto Murillo was dead, no one would pay them for the killing. Bullets for the automatic rifles were expensive and the cost came from the policemen's own salaries.

"Hold it!" he said to the others. "Don't shoot!"

When Diamante gave him a questioning look, he explained about the likelihood of their labor being unrewarded. He added, "If we stick around any longer, someone is going to drive by and see us. And if someone sees us, we're going to have to investigate what happened down there. It looks very complicated. It is very hot. It could take many hours."

Diamante mopped his face with his shirttail. "It's too hot for complicated," he said.

"Then let's get the hell out of here," Mandelo said.

WHEN GRIMALDI touched the plane down, Bolan and the boys were busting through the brush onto the road. By the time he got the Cessna turned and stopped, they were right behind him. Bolan led the boys around the tail, through the prop wind, to the passenger door, which he opened.

"*Buenas tardes,*" Grimaldi said, grinning to beat the band.

"Thanks for the help," Bolan said.

"My pleasure, Striker."

Bolan tipped forward the copilot's chair and helped the boys into the back. As soon as the Executioner took the front seat, Grimaldi released the brakes. The Cessna rapidly picked up speed, jarring violently over ruts. Then it lifted off into smooth air.

They had climbed about twenty feet when bullets sped past the windshield into the front of the single wing.

"It looks like we missed one," Grimaldi said, pointing ahead.

Through the front windshield, Bolan saw a man kneeling, shooting from the middle of the road. He recognized him at once. It was Roberto Murillo.

The Executioner dug a grenade from the crate at his feet and yanked the safety pin. "Give me an angle," he said to Grimaldi as he slid back the window in his door.

As they passed to the left of the kneeling figure, Bolan flipped the grenade out the window.

ROBERTO MURILLO wasn't thinking about anything but bringing down the plane. He fired a series of short bursts, aiming at the windshield and propeller. Because his bad leg had forced him to kneel, his shooting stance was weak. He couldn't control the muzzle climb on full auto. Most of his bullets sailed high, above the target.

Apparently undamaged, the Cessna swept over him. And as it did, another dark object dropped from it. Murillo knew what it was this time. He turned and hopped. Hopped like a maniac.

The explosion blew him sideways and sent him crashing to the road. He knew he'd been badly hit. The left side of his face had no feeling in it, nor did his left arm. He struggled up on his right elbow. Blood poured off his jaw, dripping into the dirt. His left arm had been sliced open in a dozen places.

The only sound was the steady drone of the plane as it turned north and climbed over the bay.

Murillo rolled to his back on the sand. He whimpered. The veil of shock was slowly lifting, replaced by jolts of white-hot pain. A thousand feet overhead, he saw a flock of buzzards circled against the blue sky, riding the desert thermals.

Soon, they would pick out the scent of death from below.

Soon, they would spiral down and land on the chests of the fallen. The helpless. With claws and beaks, and flapping dark wings, they would fight over the eyes.

His eyes.

23

When the numbers fell to zero, Ramon Murillo's troopers kicked open the rear doors of the moving van and poured out onto the street. They'd had so many dry runs on the operation that now, facing the real thing, they were loose, alert and eager.

Half the force crossed the wide boulevard on a dead run. They reached the mansion's high block wall, then moved along it toward the gate. The other half of the unit sprinted up the street and made for the avenue's tree-lined center divider directly opposite the gates. The two men carrying LAW rockets knelt beside the bases of the palm trees, extended the firing tubes and shouldered the launchers.

On the far side of the gate, a lone guard in a plaid sports shirt stepped into view. He took one look at the men in full combat armor positioned across the street and whirled for cover, grabbing at the communications device clipped to his belt.

The LAW rockets were released.

HEAT warheads hit the seam between the two gates. The explosion was tremendous. It ripped the gate apart, tearing the steel hinges from the concrete support posts. Ten-foot pieces of gate windmilled into the two vans that blocked the driveway.

Before the smoke cleared, before all the flying debris had hit the ground, the troopers had tossed aside the spent LAW launch tubes and picked up new ones. The second set of rockets screeched across the street. Their high explosive warheads blew the two vans into heaps of scrap metal in the process, tipping one over on its side.

The hired guns swept across the road and along the wall, rejoining at the ruined gate. As they spilled through onto the grounds, they were set upon by the pack of rottweilers.

The big dogs didn't bark. They attacked, leaping up, seizing the men's armored forearms in their jaws, shaking their heads, trying to pull their victims to the ground.

The troopers worked in pairs. One man occupied a dog's attention by letting it gnaw his protected arm, while the other got in position and took aim with a handgun. Single shots cracked, as one after another, each of the animals was quickly dispatched.

As two members of the assault force charged the mansion's front doors, a head appeared in the second story window.

Head, torso, pistol.

Someone yelled a warning.

From the cover of the wrecked vans, a third of Murillo's troops opened fire, shattering the window, hammering the facing of the frame, chewing divots in the finely chiseled white stone. They sprayed the other front-facing windows as well, keeping the men inside from firing, allowing their two compadres to safely reach the doors.

When they got there, they worked fast, placing small explosive charges in the corners of the door frame, then ducking for cover around either side of the entrance.

With a boom and a rolling cloud of smoke, the tall double doors crashed inward, blown off their hinges. The smoke was still pouring out as the troopers swarmed inside, looking for someone to kill.

HAL BROGNOLA was standing in an upstairs room, updating the President on the situation via a secure phone line when the whole building rocked violently. The tall windows shattered inward. The floor rippled underfoot, staggering him. He threw out a hand, catching hold of the desktop to keep from falling. Before he could drop the phone, the second set of explosions ripped the air, forcing him to grab for support again.

The Secret Service man in the room with him somehow managed to pick himself up off the floor, clear his weapon and jump to the emptied window frame. Before he could open fire, a fusillade of automatic fire raged through the opening. Hit at least a dozen times in the chest and head, the man stumbled backwards and crashed down amid the broken glass.

"Shit!" Brognola said, picking up the man's dropped mini-Uzi. His worst nightmare had come true. They were under an all-out attack.

He ducked from the room as more autofire stitched across the back wall. When he reached the hallway, the floor shuddered under another explosion. This one was muffled, not as powerful, but almost directly below him.

He groaned. The front doors! If they were through the front doors, his route to the elevator was blocked. Brognola reversed direction and ran down the corridor.

In front of him, two bodyguards stepped from a doorway. He shouted at them as he ran past, "Come with me!"

When they got to the stairwell at the back of the building, Brognola stopped, puffing from the exertion. "Get on the horn!" he told one of the Secret Service agents. "Tell the guys in the bunker I'm coming down. Prepare them for a full-scale retreat."

As the man unclipped his walkie-talkie, Brognola started down the stairs. Automatic fire blistered from the front of the house. An all-out gun battle. He came around the first landing with the mini-Uzi out front, ready to rip.

There was no one below him.

When he reached the ground floor, it was a different story. The corridor seethed with back-and-forth volleys of gunfire. A quick look to his right told him a pair of Secret Service guys had position in the doorways closest to the elevator. The elevator doors were open. Another agent was firing from inside, sticking his weapon out around the corner and fanning the corridor.

"Hey!" the big Fed shouted at them over the din. "It's Brognola. Give me some covering fire!"

When the massed weapons opened up, pinning the opposition at the far end of the hall, Brognola darted out, and running as low as he could, he dived into the elevator car. He jumped up at once. "Come on!" he said to the men across the hall. "Get in here!"

He poked the stubby snout of the mini-Uzi around the elevator entrance and fired a series of short bursts, covering his security team. When they were safely in the car, Brognola jammed a thumb on the down button.

Over the rattle of gunfire came an incongruously sweet chime and the elevator doors hissed closed.

Not a second too soon.

Outside the car, Brognola could hear heavy feet running down the hallway toward them.

The motor engaged and the car began to descend.

When the elevator stopped and the doors opened, Brognola told one of the men, "Stay in the car. Keep the doors open. Don't let it go back up."

Two more armed men stood waiting for him in the corridor. The heavyset one with a salt-and-pepper crew cut was Brunell, the security chief.

"Is this everyone?" Brognola asked him.

"Kline and Baxter are with the witness," Brunell said. "It looks like we've got eight, total, on this level."

"Let's pull back to the exit," Brognola said.

As they turned to go, autofire screamed down through the elevator shaft, through the car's roof and ricocheted off the floor, sending them all scattering. The man guarding the car was caught in a hail of bullets. Hit in the head and back, he collapsed inside.

Before anyone could reach them, the elevator doors closed. With a chime and a clunk, the car started up.

"We've got to move, people!" Brognola said, as he started down the corridor. "They'll be on top of us in a couple of minutes."

Brognola stuck his head in the open conference-room door. Yovana Ortiz was standing. Over her dress, she was wearing an armored vest with steel trauma plates. She looked very scared.

"It's the Murillos, isn't it?" she said. "They've come for me."

Above them, the muffled sounds of gunfire were rapidly dwindling. A sign that the agents upstairs were no longer putting up a fight, which meant they were wounded or dead.

Brognola didn't answer her question. "We can't stay here any longer," he told her. "We have a safe escape route and we're going to use it."

When Ortiz stepped out into the hall, the whole crew moved with her. They hustled down the bleak, gray corridor with the witness in the middle of the pack.

As they rounded a turn Brognola heard a chime sound. Behind them the elevator doors had opened. He started to shout a warning when the world jolted. The shock wave was a hundred times worse than what he'd felt upstairs. The hallway floor flew up and smashed him in the face, the walls played ping-pong with his body. A choking rush of concrete dust whooshed over him as behind them, a huge section of the corridor ceiling came crashing down.

When the shaking stopped, and the dimmed overhead lights came back to full strength, Brognola scrambled to his feet and found Ortiz. She seemed dazed but otherwise unhurt as he helped her up.

"Fuckers are trying to bury us alive!" Brunell spit.

"Chief, where's Kline?" one of the agents said. "He was right behind me."

It didn't take long to find him. His hand was sticking out of the rubble of the ceiling. The fingers weren't moving. Brunell and the others hurried to lift the concrete chunks off the man. They stopped when they had exposed his head. It was caved in.

"We've got to get out of here!" Brognola said. Then he shouted at the others, "Go! Go!"

They raced another 150 feet down the corridor to a steel, bulkhead door with a heavy, triple-cross bolt locking system. It took two men to unlock it and three to pull it open.

A shaft of muted sunlight shot into the tunnel. On the other side of the door was a six-foot, corrugated drain pipe.

Two abreast, with Ortiz again in the middle, they rushed through the pipe, toward a much brighter light.

Outside the afternoon was sunny and quite warm. And there was no sign of danger.

The instant they cleared the exit, Brunell took the lead, moving downhill to the footpath that skirted the base of the bluff. As the security team followed, they held their weapons ready. When they reached the path, they traveled single file at a fast pace. Despite the heavy body armor, Ortiz kept up with the men. Brognola brought up the rear, constantly looking over his shoulder, making sure that they hadn't been followed out of the tunnel.

Ahead of them were the gaudy canopies and pennants of the public market. The place was packed with milling people. As far as Brognola could tell, the shoppers seemed unaware of what was happening on the mesa. Maybe the gunfire and explosions had sounded like fireworks to them. Maybe the loud mariachi music partially veiled the noise. Those shoppers who happened to look over at the footpath, at the line of armed, running men and the lone woman, kept on looking because the sight was so unusual.

Slowing the column to a fast walk at the edge of the

market, Brunell used his communications device to warn the team manning the escape van that they were en route with the witness and had been under hostile fire.

As they hurriedly crossed a makeshift dining area, Brognola scanned the faces of the people standing and sitting around the little tables. His eyes moved past a gaunt man with slicked-back hair wearing dark glasses and a sour expression.

"Yovana!" a shrill voice cried out.

An elderly woman in a peasant costume rushed headlong at them. She held a bouquet of red roses clutched in her hands. The Secret Service men reacted instantly. They turned and aimed their pistols at her.

"Stop!" Brunell shouted.

But the old woman ignored the guns pointing at her head and threw herself at Ortiz.

"God, don't shoot her!" Ortiz cried. "Are you crazy? She just wants an autograph!"

The bodyguards held their fire, which allowed the old woman to heave her saggy-fleshed arms around the younger, taller woman's neck. The woman embraced her fiercely, pulling up hard against the armored vest and its trauma plates.

Ortiz returned the embrace, out of self-defense. As she did, her fingers touched something lumpy and strange under the woman's embroidered dress. Puzzled, she stared down at the old woman's face, at her sad, desperate, resigned expression.

"It is for my children," the old woman said. "I'm sorry, but you understand."

An instant before Yovana Ortiz started to struggle against the bear hug, Brognola's eyes snapped back to the seated man, who was now smiling. A man he recognized as Ramon Murillo. "No!" Brognola shouted. "No!"

The power of the explosion drowned out his warning and rocked the ground underfoot. The blast thrust the embracing women apart. In a flash of blinding light, it tore the old woman to pieces, literally limb from limb. It sent Ortiz flying backward thirty feet. She landed on her back in the dirt.

Brognola rushed to her side. He could see at once, and to his horror, that the armored vest had only protected her torso. Brognola knelt. Looking down at the bloody ruin of her face, at her grotesquely mangled arms and legs, he was sure she was already dead.

Then she opened her eyes.

"My children," she said softly. "Protect my children."

Brognola felt something warm against his thigh. Arterial blood was jetting from both her legs, spraying across his trousers. He tried frantically to slow it with hand pressure. There was no way to stop it.

"The evidence, Yovana," he said. "Where is it? You don't have much time."

She spoke again. Her words were so faint, he had to put his ear to her lips in order to hear them. Her final breath brushed his cheek.

EPILOGUE

When the radio transmission came in from Hal Brognola, the Cessna was cruising on autopilot at five thousand feet, following the coastline up the west side of the Sea of Cortez. Near the horizon, beyond the town of San Felipe, the sea ended in an estuary, fed by the Colorado River. Tijuana was still almost two hundred miles away, on the other side of the Baja.

Mack Bolan stopped studying the view out his window and watched as Jack Grimaldi flipped a switch on the dash and spoke into his headset microphone. "Blackjack here, go ahead, Hal. Over."

"Are the children safe? Over."

"This is Striker, Hal," Bolan said, "The boys are A-okay. Over."

The combination of the strain they had been under, the smooth air, steady engine vibration, the hot sun streaming in through the Cessna's windows had made the boys drowsy. They had both been sleeping in the back seat for better than two hours.

"And you? Over."

"Blackjack is fine. So am I. Over."

Then Brognola said, "If the children have got their headsets on, please take them out of the loop. Over."

The tone of his voice, even through the static of the radio signal, told Bolan that something had gone wrong at the Tijuana end. Very wrong. "They're not in the loop, Hal.

Over,'' he said. The boys were wearing their headsets to muffle the considerable engine noise in the cabin, but Grimaldi had disabled the earphones so they could sleep.

When Brognola told them what had just happened in Tijuana, Grimaldi said, ''Jesus!''

''There was nothing we could do,'' Brognola continued. ''They attacked us in force, with heavy explosives and they had our retreat blocked off. They used a decoy to get close to the Ortiz woman. A suicider. It was Ramon Murillo's handiwork. Over.''

''Who's going to tell the kids? Over,'' Grimaldi asked.

After a long pause, Brognola said, ''My job. I'll do it, after you land in Tijuana. What is your ETA? Over.''

''We're about two hours away. Over,'' Grimaldi replied.

The Executioner looked around his seat at the brothers, peacefully sleeping with arms entwined. The little guys had come through so much hell, so bravely. The trouble was, for them the hell had only just begun. The last thing he had said to them before they conked out was, ''Don't worry. You'll be with your mama in a few hours.''

Those words now stuck deep in his craw.

''That's a no-go, Hal,'' Bolan said. ''The kids are expecting their mother to meet them at the airport. There's no way I'm going to let their hopes continue to build. It'd be even more devastating to them if they got the news after they arrived. They're sleeping soundly, now. When they wake up, I'll break it to them myself. Over.''

''Of course, you're right, Striker, I wasn't thinking straight. I guess I'm still a bit rattled by what happened. I'll see you guys in a couple of hours. Safe landing. Over and out.''

As Grimaldi signed off, he glanced up at the tall man in the copilot's chair. Nothing but desert sun reflected back at him in the Executioner's sunglasses. Below the mask of gray-tinted, wraparound lenses, in the set of his mouth, the line of his jaw, Grimaldi sensed the power of a rising storm, of rushing dark clouds, ominous in the distance.

A hurricane was on its way.

Don't miss Executioner #260,
DAYHUNT, Volume II in the exciting
LORD OF THE SEAS TRILOGY.

JAMES AXLER

DEATH LANDS®

Pandora's Redoubt

Ryan Cawdor and his fellow survivalists emerge in a redoubt in which they discover a sleek superarmored personnel carrier bristling with weapons from predark days. As the companions leave the redoubt, a sudden beeping makes them realize why the builders were constructing a supermachine in the first place.

Desperate times call for desperate measures. Don't miss out on the action in these titles!

#61910	FLASHBACK	$5.50 U.S.	☐
		$6.50 CAN.	☐
#61911	ASIAN STORM	$5.50 U.S.	☐
		$6.50 CAN.	☐
#61912	BLOOD STAR	$5.50 U.S.	☐
		$6.50 CAN.	☐
#61913	EYE OF THE RUBY	$5.50 U.S.	☐
		$6.50 CAN.	☐
#61914	VIRTUAL PERIL	$5.50 U.S.	☐
		$6.50 CAN.	☐

(limited quantities available on certain titles)

TOTAL AMOUNT	$
POSTAGE & HANDLING	$
($1.00 for one book, 50¢ for each additional)	
APPLICABLE TAXES*	$ _____
TOTAL PAYABLE	$ _____

(check or money order—please do not send cash)

To order, complete this form and send it, along with a check or money order for the total above, payable to Gold Eagle Books, to: **In the U.S.:** 3010 Walden Avenue, P.O. Box 9077, Buffalo, NY 14269-9077; **In Canada:** P.O. Box 636, Fort Erie, Ontario, L2A 5X3.

Name: _____

Address: _____ City: _____

State/Prov.: _____ Zip/Postal Code: _____

*New York residents remit applicable sales taxes.
 Canadian residents remit applicable GST and provincial taxes.

GOLD EAGLE

GSMBACK1

Journey back to the future with these classic

DEATH LANDS®

titles!

James Axler

OUTLANDERS®

HELL RISING

A fierce bid for power is raging throughout new empires of what was once the British Isles. The force of the apocalypse has released an ancient city, and within its vaults lies the power of total destruction. Kane must challenge the forces who would harness the weapon of the gods to wreak final destruction.

GOUT14